MW01134300

DARK MAGIC

Harbinger P.I. Book 3

ADAM J. WRIGHT

THE HARBINGER P.I. SERIES

LOST SOUL
BURIED MEMORY
DARK MAGIC

CHAPTER 1

FELICITY HELPED ME THROUGH THE front door, out of the rain and into the warmth of the house. I sat on the sofa, shivering from the cold that seemed to have permeated my skin and chilled my bones and internal organs. Felicity fussed around in the kitchen and, after a few seconds, the rich aroma of coffee drifted into the living room. It was the best smell I'd ever experienced in my life.

She came into the living room and stood with her hands on her hips. She'd wiped the rain from the lenses of her glasses and her dark eyes looked concerned. "You should take a hot shower and put some dry clothes on while I make the coffee."

I nodded, still shivering. "Felicity, what are you doing here? When I saw you at the hospital…"

"We'll talk about that after you get warmed up. Can you make it to the bathroom?"

I stood warily. At least my muscles seemed to be working again. "I'll be fine," I said. I went through the kitchen and down the hall to the bathroom. I turned the temperature dial on the shower as hot as I could get it and stepped under the scalding spray, closing my eyes and letting the water run over my face and body. It hit my skin like a thousand white-hot needles, but it felt far better than the insidious cold that had been seeping into my body.

My strength eventually returned. By the time I stepped out of the shower and wrapped a towel around my waist, I felt almost like my old self again. I went back through the house, passing Felicity in the kitchen as she was pouring coffee into two mugs, and went up to my bedroom where I put on gray sweatpants and a hoodie that had the words "Miskatonic University" across the front and "Dept of Medieval Metaphysics" across the back.

My old colleague Jim Walker, whom I'd worked with in Canada during my early days as an investigator, had bought it for me. Jim had been a big fan of H.P. Lovecraft and had given me the hoodie as a graduation present when I'd become a fully-fledged P.I. and gone solo.

When I got back downstairs, Felicity had also changed into dry clothing and was sitting on the sofa. Her luggage, which she'd left on her driveway when she'd come over to my lawn and hauled my ass inside, was now sitting inside the front door with her wet clothes on top of it. She must have gone back out to retrieve it and then changed into the black slacks and white blouse she was wearing now. Her dark hair hung around her face in damp tendrils but it looked like she'd dried it with a towel. Two steaming mugs sat on the coffee table in front of her.

"You look much better than when you were lying outside on the wet grass," she said as I sank into the easy chair and picked up a mug of coffee. "What was that all about?"

"It's a long story," I said. "Probably much longer than yours. So why don't you start? Why did you come back? When I saw you in the hospital in London, you seemed pretty certain that you were staying in England."

"Yes, I was certain at the time. There just seemed to be so much death everywhere and it made me question my career choice. Being poisoned by a demon didn't help, either. And seeing Jason again made me realize that I had options. I could lead a normal life. That was very appealing at the time. So I made a decision to stay in England and forget all about demons, and changelings, and witches." She paused to take a drink. I did the same. The hot, bitter coffee was the best I'd ever tasted.

"So what changed your mind?" I asked, holding my mug in both hands and letting the steam drift up to my face, bringing with it the rich coffee aroma.

"When I was discharged from the hospital," Felicity said, "Jason came to pick me up. He was excited because he wanted to show me a house in Essex that he was going

3

to buy for us to live in. I was still a bit too tired to want to go looking at houses but I agreed and he drove us out there. The house was lovely, a little cottage with a quaint garden and a nearby village that was like something out of an Agatha Christie novel. It was perfect."

She took another drink and set her mug down on the coffee table. "But the more I looked around the place and thought about spending my days there, the more I began to feel scared. I felt that if I spent my life in that house, in that village, I would slowly die inside. I can't explain it fully, Alec, but it was as if living a normal life was even more dangerous than working here, fighting monsters. I knew that if I tried to live the life Jason wanted me to live, I would be dead before I even knew it. Dead inside."

I nodded, understanding exactly what she meant. It was what I'd tried to explain to her on the flight to England. Felicity wasn't meant for a mundane life. She was like me, unable to turn her back on the preternatural world once she knew of its existence.

"So here I am," she said. She smiled but there was a sadness in her eyes.

"You left Jason?" I asked.

She nodded. "He made it clear that I couldn't be with him and pursue a career as an investigator as well. He said I had to make a choice between you or him, as if the situation hinged on what man I chose to be with, not what I wanted for myself. So I told him I wasn't choosing you or him, I was choosing me, making the decision I thought would be best for me and no one else. I think that shocked him even more than my decision to return here." She straightened slightly and looked proud of herself. Hell, she had every right to be. I was proud of her too.

I felt myself grinning, trying to imagine Jason's face when Felicity had stood up for herself. The self-righteous prick had tried to pay me to tell Felicity to stay in England. It must have been a shock when she dumped his ass.

"What are you grinning at?" she asked me.

"I'm just imagining you telling Jason that you're an independent woman. It probably fried the circuits in his medieval brain."

She giggled, all traces of her earlier sadness gone. It was good to see her laugh. "Now, tell me your story," she said. "Judging by the state of the Land Rover and the condition I found you in, I'd say I missed all the action."

"The state of the Land Rover? I left it at the cemetery. I drove back here in Mallory's Jeep." But now that I thought back to when Mallory had left, the Land Rover had been sitting in the driveway. At the time, I'd been too upset by Mallory's departure to give the vehicle's mysterious appearance a second thought.

"Yes," Felicity said, "it looks like you've hit another vehicle."

I got up and went to the front door. The rain had stopped, leaving the road and sidewalk glistening in the glow from the streetlights. Even in the darkness, I could see where the front of the Land Rover had been damaged

5

on the driver's side. The lights were smashed, the bodywork crumpled.

I put on my boots and went out to the vehicle, running my hand over the dented metal. "What the hell?"

"You don't remember doing it?" Felicity asked from the doorway.

"I didn't do it. Sure, I drove through a horde of zombies and crashed through the gates of the cemetery but it wasn't damaged like this."

"Zombies?"

I nodded, noticing a sheet of paper on the back seat, along with the Box of Midnight and the Land Rover keys. I opened the door and took out the paper, which was something fancy—vellum, maybe—and looked at the words written on it in an ornate script. I read them aloud.

"Alec, I thought you might not want the police to find this at the cemetery, so I returned it for you. Unfortunately, I had a slight mishap on the way to your house. Crashed into a brick wall. I'll never get used to these newfangled automobiles. Sorry about that." The message was signed with an ornate "P". "It's from Polidori," I said.

"Polidori?" Felicity frowned in confusion.

"John Polidori," I said, taking the blackened Box of Midnight and my car keys out of the vehicle before locking it.

"The same John Polidori who knew Byron and wrote *The Vampyre* in 1816?"

"Is that when he wrote it? Yeah, that's him." I went back into the house and placed the Box of Midnight on the coffee table, along with Polidori's note.

Felicity picked up the mugs. "So you drove through a horde of zombies, and a physician from the nineteenth century crashed your Land Rover. I'll make some more coffee. You have a lot of explaining to do."

CHAPTER 2

THE BUZZING OF MY PHONE woke me the next morning. I reached over to the nightstand and picked it up, groaning inwardly when I saw the office number on the screen. Why the hell was Felicity there so early? I answered the call and she began speaking before I even got a chance to say hello.

"Alec, you need to get down here right away."

"I do?" I asked, trying to make out the time on the bedside clock through blurry eyes. "Why? What time is it?"

"It's half past ten. The sheriff has been here this morning, looking for you. He was going to come to your house but I told him you'd be here shortly."

"Is he there now?"

"No, he had to go somewhere but said he'd be back shortly. You need to come to the office, Alec."

"All right, give me ten minutes." I ended the call and slid out of bed, hoping a shower would wake me up. Felicity and I had stayed up until the early hours discussing the events in London and what had happened in Dearmont last night. She had been genuinely upset when I told her about Mallory destroying the Box of Midnight and cursing herself with only a year to live.

I hadn't mentioned the magical blast I'd used to kill DuMont at the cemetery. I was still too confused about that to talk about it openly. I wanted to wait and see if any more memories came back to me that might explain why I had been able to do that to DuMont. I was also trying to figure out why my father had taken me to the Coven when I was a child and had them cast an enchantment on me.

Until I could figure out more, I wasn't going to burden Felicity with my problems. She had enough of her own to deal with. Yes, she'd left Jason and come back to Maine but I knew it wasn't going to be so cut and dried as that. Felicity would probably experience an emotional rollercoaster for a while. I would be here for her when that happened.

She'd said she would help me research the curse that had been attached to the Box of Midnight and would try to find a way to reverse it. I wasn't about to give up on Mallory.

I had no idea where Mallory was and, even though that wasn't unusual, I was concerned because she'd taken off while still trying to come to terms with Rekhmire's curse.

It probably wasn't a good idea for her to be alone right now. She needed support, even if she wouldn't admit it.

Going on a desperate search for Mister Scary when she had no leads was only going to end in disappointment. She was a strong girl but dealing with Rekhmire's curse and the fact that she was no closer to finding the killer responsible for the Bloody Summer Night Massacre would be enough to break anyone.

I made a decision to call Mallory later. Even if she wouldn't come back here, having someone to talk to might help her figure out her next move. She was my friend and I wanted to help her any way I could. Besides, she had taken that curse to help me defeat DuMont's zombie army.

I showered and dressed quickly and went outside to inspect the damaged Land Rover in daylight. The morning was bright, the sun already burning off the moisture from last night's downpour. The damage to the Land Rover's bodywork was mainly cosmetic apart from the smashed light, which I would have to get fixed today. I didn't want to give Sheriff Cantrell a reason to give me a ticket. He was probably going to throw the book at me for last night's zombie attack on the town anyway.

I drove in town and parked in my usual place, next to Felicity's blue Mini, behind the building that housed my office. I walked onto Main Street but didn't make it to my office door because Cantrell intercepted me outside Dearmont Donuts.

"Harbinger," he said gruffly, coming out of the donut shop with a bright green box under his arm, "I need to speak with you."

"Of course," I said, putting on a smile and a cheery voice. "How can I help you today, Sheriff?"

"Don't give me that shit-eating grin, Harbinger. You don't think I've had enough of your bullshit after what happened last night?" He pointed at the door that bore the words HARBINGER P.I. and said, "Your office. Now."

I opened the door for him and followed his considerable bulk up the narrow stairs to my office. As I passed Felicity's door, I gave her a little wave. She was working on her computer, her hair piled up on her head and an expression of concentration on her face. She looked damned good for someone who had only caught a few hours of sleep last night. When she saw me, she waved back and went to the coffee maker.

Cantrell settled into one of the chairs at the desk and I went around to my own, larger chair. "Felicity will be bringing coffee in a minute," I told him. "Are you going to break out the donuts or are they for your colleagues at the station?"

He glared at me. "You think you're a real wise guy, don't you, Harbinger? You're lucky I don't throw your ass in jail for what happened last night."

"And what exactly happened last night, Sheriff?" I sat back in my chair, waiting for his answer.

His face fell a little. "Well, we don't know yet exactly. But people were busting out of their graves in South Cemetery and walking up Main Street." He recovered his composure and pointed a meaty finger at me. "Don't try and tell me that was nothing to do with you. I know what your job entails; meddling with things that shouldn't concern normal people. You're playing with fire and it's the good people of this town who are getting burned."

"Was anyone hurt last night?" I asked him. I knew that what happened was DuMont's fault but if anyone had been injured, I was going to feel guilty about it.

"Only minor injuries," Cantrell said. "Luckily, those walking skeletons were easily killed." He frowned at his own words. "I can't believe I just said that. Zombies belong in books and movies, Harbinger, not on the streets of Dearmont. I'm the sheriff of a small town; I shouldn't have to deal with the undead."

"No, you shouldn't," I agreed. "That's my job."

The door opened and Felicity came in, carrying a tray of coffee and donuts. I recognized the donuts as coming from Dearmont Donuts, the same as the ones Cantrell had. So Felicity hadn't had time to bake something from scratch this morning; she was human after all.

She placed the tray on my desk without a word and went back to the door.

Cantrell turned slightly in his seat to address her. "You may want to stay, Miss Lake. I didn't just come here to ball out your boss." He sighed resignedly. "I came to offer him a job."

Felicity turned to face us and I expected her to look as surprised as I felt at hearing Cantrell's words, but her British composure kept her features unreadable. "I'll get my notebook," she said.

Cantrell sat quietly until she returned. I was in a state of stunned silence. The sheriff hated me, so why the hell would he hire me to do a job for him? There was the matter of his dead wife's involvement with a church where she and twelve other people had been murdered, of course, but as far as Cantrell and the other authorities were concerned, the perpetrator of that crime had been my predecessor, Sherry Westlake.

When Felicity took a seat at the end of the desk and opened her notebook to a fresh page, I asked Cantrell, "What can I do for you, Sheriff?"

"There's an old case," he said. "In fact, it's three years old and as far as my department is concerned, it's a cold case but I keep thinking there might be something we missed at the time. I suspect the case might involve…things in your area of expertise. I didn't think so at the time but my thinking about such matters has changed over the intervening years."

"You mean the case of the lady in the lake," I said, remembering the news report I'd read online when I'd first seen a picture of Sheriff Cantrell and his daughter, Amy.

He looked surprised. "Yes, I am talking about that. But Deirdre Summers' body isn't in Dearmont Lake. We sent search parties out there in boats and we sent divers down into the depths looking for her. There was no body."

"You don't think she might have simply left town and left her clothes by the lake to make it look like suicide?" I asked.

He shook his head. "No, I don't. Deirdre was as straight-laced as they come. For her to disappear like that, there had to be foul play involved." He paused, as if considering what to say next. When he spoke again, he said, "I'll have someone bring over the case file. When you read it, you'll see why I think the case might be best investigated by someone in your line of work."

I wondered if the sheriff had shown the file to Sherry Westlake. With the case being so old, it was possible. I took a shot in the dark. "Have you shown the case file to any other preternatural investigators?"

A dark look crossed his face. "No, I have not."

"I'll be happy to take a look," I said, changing the subject. It was obvious that Cantrell was thinking of Sherry Westlake, the woman he thought had murdered his wife. Hell, for all I knew, she had murdered his wife but I didn't want the sheriff dwelling on it in my office. He had a gun, after all, and he seemed to have tarred all P.I.s with the same brush as Sherry Westlake. I was still shocked that he was hiring me to look into the Deirdre Summers case.

"I have to ask," I said, "why are you hiring me, Sheriff? You don't like me, that much is obvious. So why come to me with this?"

"You're right, I don't like you. And after the events of last night, I like you even less." He leaned across the desk slightly, his weight pushing it across the floor toward me. "But I can rise above my personal feelings to do my job. Deirdre Summers was a respected member of this community and she left behind a daughter who has no idea what happened to her mother. I owe it to that young lady to solve the case of her mother's death, even if it means working with people like you."

"Fair enough," I said. We were obviously never going to be friends but if he was willing to put our differences aside and work with me on a professional level, then I would do the same. "I have another case I'm working on, so I'll add the Deirdre Summers case to my workload just as soon as I can take a look at that case file." I didn't mention that the other case I was working on was an investigation into the church his wife had attended. Nor did I tell him that his daughter had hired me to look into the church and his wife's death.

"I assume I'm being paid by the Sheriff's Department for this investigation?" I said.

Cantrell nodded. "You'll be paid as a consultant. That means I want to see detailed breakdowns of your time and expenses."

"Of course. Felicity will handle that. Am I to report any developments in the case to you?"

He grinned at me like a wolf looking at a trapped rabbit. "You won't be reporting to me, Harbinger, I'll be working the case with you."

The shock I felt must have registered on my face because Cantrell's grin widened.

"No," I said. "I work with Felicity."

"Not on this case." He pointed at me with a huge finger. "You think I'm going to let you handle police business on your own? I'm going to be keeping a close eye on you every step of the way."

This was going to be a nightmare. I would be working with Cantrell on the Deirdre Summers case while also investigating the death of his wife without his knowledge. I wanted to say no and send him on his way but what choice did I have? If I declined the case, he was going to start getting pissy about last night's zombie attack and I'd probably end up in jail.

I sighed. "Okay, I'll work the case with you," I said, my voice sounding even more resigned than I'd intended. I'd wanted to suggest that I wasn't happy about the arrangement but my tone made it sound like I was a condemned man about to leave his cell for the final time.

"Don't think I'm looking forward to this any more than you are," he said. "But Deirdre died on my watch and I will not allow the case to remain unsolved, even if it means working with the likes of you."

I wasn't in the mood to take a barrage of insults. I wanted Cantrell out of my office so I would have time to think without him looming over me. I stood up. "I'll need to read the case file before we get started."

He stood too and gave me a curt nod. "I'll send someone over with it this morning." He offered his hand reluctantly, as if he were about to place it in something nasty. I shook it, making sure to grip his hand tightly and look into his eyes. The fact that he'd offered his hand despite his dislike of me told me that he'd been brought up with traditional values and that meant he would respect a strong handshake with eye contact.

He released my hand and nodded to Felicity. "Miss Lake, thank you for the coffee." He turned and left. I heard the stairs groan beneath his weight as he went downstairs. Then the main door opened and closed and I watched him through the window as he went to his patrol car and put his box of donuts into the passenger side before climbing into the driver's seat and starting the engine. He drove south along Main Street toward the police station.

"Well, I wasn't expecting that," I told Felicity.

"No, neither was I. At least we have more work. There's always room for another case."

"Yeah," I agreed. "Except I have to work it with Sheriff Cantrell."

"Maybe that's a good thing. This could be an opportunity for you to earn his trust. He might give you more consultancy jobs if you bond with him."

"Bond with him? We're not going on a boys' night out, we're investigating a woman's death. Besides, he hates me and that isn't going to change any time soon."

She shrugged. "Maybe he'll learn to trust you."

"Trust me? While I'm working with him on the Deirdre Summers case, I'll be investigating his wife's death behind his back. That isn't the foundation of a trusting relationship."

"Well I think it's good that he already trusts you enough to bring you this case."

"It isn't that he trusts me," I told her. "He wants to keep an eye on me. He said so himself. I wonder what he's up to."

Felicity stood up and smoothed her skirt before picking up her notebook. "I'm sure you boys will stop fighting one day and play nice. I'll be in my office if you need me."

"I need you now," I said, then realized how that sounded and added, "We should drive over to Clara and take a look at that church."

"We have to wait for the sheriff to send the Deirdre Summers case file over," she reminded me.

"Nah, we can collect it on the way. No point sitting around in the office waiting for it to arrive. Let's go." I picked up my keys and headed for the door. I was eager to get started on a case and give my mind something to occupy itself with that didn't involve cursed friends or mysterious powers. I wanted to lose myself in the investigations of the church and Deirdre Summers' disappearance.

"I'll need to change first," she said. "I'm not rummaging around an old abandoned church in heels."

"Okay, should we drop by your place so you can grab something?"

"No need. I'll be back in a minute." She left the room and a couple of seconds later I heard her office door close. When she reappeared a few minutes later, she was wearing sneakers, jeans, and a light green, tight T-shirt.

I got up and grabbed my car keys again before it became too obvious that I was staring at her. But damn, she looked hot.

"Shouldn't we take my car?" Felicity asked. "Your Land Rover is smashed up, remember?"

"It isn't that bad. I drove it here."

"Still, you really should get it repaired."

I sighed. She was right. "Okay, I'll find a mechanic."

"There's a place on the highway called Earl's Autos. It's in the direction we're going."

"Okay, we'll drop the Land Rover there on the way to Clara." I went downstairs and out onto Main Street, Felicity close behind me. I locked up and we walked around the building to the parking spaces at the rear.

Felicity held up her key fob and pressed it. The lights on the blue Mini flashed once and the locks clicked open.

"We should put the weapons in my car before we take yours to the garage," she said. "We wouldn't want a mechanic finding your enchanted sword."

I pointed at her little blue car. "Is everything going to fit inside there?"

Felicity shot me an exasperated look. "It's not that small, Alec. The earlier models were much smaller than this."

I shrugged and opened up the back of the Land Rover. There was no way the weapons and tools of the trade that I carried around were all going to fit in Felicity's Mini. I took out the daggers and sword and transferred them to her trunk, along with a couple of bags of salt, my Victorian vampire hunter's kit, my shotgun, and a shovel. I had no idea how long the Land Rover would be in the shop, so I had to make sure I was covered for every eventuality. For all I knew, the church at Clara could house a nest of vampires and the innocent-looking Dearmont Lake might be the lair of a lake monster. I added my fishing tackle box to the stuff in the Mini. The box held chalk, candles, and a few herbal potions that were mostly just glass jars of mold now. I also threw my portable GPS in with everything else.

When the Mini's trunk was full, Felicity said, "See? I told you it would all fit."

"Yeah, that's great," I said, climbing into the Land Rover. I just hoped I wouldn't need to find something fast in that chaotic jumble. I didn't want to be searching through a mess of stuff, trying to find a dagger, while a troll was gnawing on my leg. "I'll meet you at the police station," I said.

Felicity followed me south along Main Street to the low building that served as the police station. There were four police cruisers in the parking lot, which I guessed was the sum total of Dearmont's Sheriff's Department. A small town like this didn't require much policing, as long as you didn't count the time zombies burst out of their graves and came shambling down Main Street.

Felicity waited in her car while I went inside the station. I pushed through a set of large glass doors that led into a reception area manned by a young deputy. He was tapping away on a computer keyboard. Behind him, three other deputies, including Amy Cantrell, were sitting at desks in the bullpen.

Amy saw me and came over. "Hey," she said. "What are you doing here?" She looked tired, as if she hadn't slept last night. With all the chaos in town, she probably hadn't. In fact, all the deputies had the same tired look. They'd probably spent all night cleaning up Main Street, taking skeletons back to South Cemetery, where they would have found even more skeletons and open graves.

"I came by to collect a case file. The Deirdre Summers case. The sheriff wanted me to take a look at it."

Her face brightened. "Yeah, he said he was going to get you to work with him and look into it. That's real good progress for him, to hire you after what happened to my mom."

21

"You don't find it strange?"

She frowned. "No, what do you mean?"

"Your dad hates me. And last night, the town was attacked by zombies, which he blames me for. You don't think it's weird that the next morning, he's in my office offering me a job?"

Amy shrugged. "Maybe it means he's finally dealing with the death of my mom. It's a step forward. When the massacre at the church happened and all clues pointed to Sherry Westlake, my dad went a little crazy trying to find her. He pulled in favors from every law enforcement department in the area.

"When it was obvious that the trail was cold, he fell into a deep depression. I wasn't sure he was ever going to shake it off. But gradually, he did. And now he's willing to work with you on the Deirdre Summers case. Maybe he'll put aside his hatred for preternatural investigators and learn to trust you."

"Yeah, everyone keeps saying that," I said.

"Oh? Who else said it?"

"Felicity."

"Well, we're right."

I shrugged. "Yeah, I'm not so sure."

Amy shook her head at me. "You don't need to be so suspicious."

"Being suspicious has kept me alive this long."

"Wait here." She went over to her desk and picked up a slim manila folder. She came back and handed it to me

22

over the counter. "That's the Summers file. There isn't much in there."

I held it up "The sheriff said there was something in here that might suggest a preternatural angle."

"Yeah, there is. You'll know it when you see it." She shrugged again. "It might mean nothing but I'm glad you're taking a look anyway. Natalie deserves to know what happened to her mother. And if there's a bad guy involved, he needs to be brought to justice."

"Natalie," I said. "Where can I find her if I need to speak with her?"

"She works at the library, same as her mom did. They used to work there together before Deirdre disappeared."

"Okay, thanks. I'll let you know if I find anything useful." I lowered my voice and said, "I'm heading over to Clara to take a look at that church."

"Just make sure my dad doesn't find out about that."

"I'll keep it from him as if my life depended on it." I went back out to the parking lot and held up the case file to show Felicity. She gave me a thumbs-up from inside her car and rolled down the window.

"Follow me to Earl's. I know the way."

I nodded and passed her the case file through the open window. "I guess we should put this in your car." She placed it on her back seat. Her little car was much tidier than the Land Rover, that was for sure.

I got into the Land Rover and followed Felicity south along Main Street. A few minutes later, we were on the highway and I could see Dearmont Lake through the trees. It looked peaceful enough, its surface shimmering brightly in the late morning sunlight. There were boats out on the water, mainly fishermen trolling for black bass, and a couple of pleasure craft.

A densely-wooded island sat out near the middle of the lake. I wondered if the police had searched it after Deirdre Summers' disappearance and immediately knew that they must have. Sheriff Cantrell might be a pain in the ass but he was thorough. The fact that he was still investigating Deirdre Summers' disappearance, long after many other sheriffs might have forgotten about it, told me he how tenacious he was. He'd gone as far as sending divers into the lake to look for the librarian's body, so he would definitely have had the island searched too.

As I drove on, the trees obscured my view of the shimmering water and I turned my attention back to the road.

Up ahead, I could see a sign that said *Earl's Autos* and an assortment of old cars in a dusty-looking parking lot. Felicity turned into the lot and I followed, parking by a long building that served as an office at one end and a workshop at the other. The cars in the lot were a variety of models, and some of them looked like they dated back to the seventies, but all of them looked lovingly maintained and cared-for, polished paintwork and chrome gleaming in the sunlight.

In the workshop, a white Honda Civic was up on a ramp and there was a guy in dark blue coveralls beneath it, draining oil from the engine into a pan on the floor.

The office door bore a sticker that read *WELCOME*. Felicity and I went inside, into a small room with an old leather sofa and a wooden coffee table weighed down by stacks of car magazines.

A window on the back wall looked out to a junkyard full of wrecked cars and trucks. Some of the automobile remains looked like they'd been rotting out there since the sixties.

Containers of anti-freeze, oil, and windshield washer fluid sat on a wire rack running along one wall. There was a counter at the far end of the room with a door behind it that I assumed led to the workshop. The reception area smelled of rubber, grease, and cigarette smoke. A lemon-scented car air freshener had been hung over the counter but its scent was lost among the other, stronger smells.

The door opened and a large lady in her fifties came to the counter. She had short blond hair and wore dark blue coveralls that matched the ones worn by the mechanic beneath the Civic. Her name, June, was embroidered on the left breast in white script. Her brown eyes flickered from me to Felicity and back to me again. "What can I do for you folks today?"

"I've got a beat-up Land Rover that needs fixing," I said.

"Sure, let's take a look." She came around the counter and followed us out to the dusty parking lot. Standing with her hands on her hips, she inspected the damage on the vehicle. "Looks like you drove it into a brick wall."

"Not me," I said. "Someone else."

June's eyes fixed on Felicity accusingly.

"Not me either," Felicity said defensively.

"Well, I'm sure we can fix it for you," June said. She turned toward the workshop and shouted, "Earl!"

The guy who had been draining the Civic came over, wiping his hands on an oily cloth. He had close-cropped gray hair and a matching beard. His frame was wiry beneath the coveralls. "Morning," he said, nodding at us.

"What do you think of this?" June asked him.

"Looks like it's been driven into a wall."

"That's what I said," she told him.

"Can you fix it?" I asked.

He nodded, eyes fixed on the crumpled bodywork. "Yeah, I can fix it but I may have to order a new light. Unless I can find a Land Rover in the yard with a light that isn't busted up."

"How long will it take?" I asked.

"If I order a new light, it'll be a couple of days. If I go searching in the yard, maybe less. Depends if I find a suitable replacement or not. If not, then I'll need to order a new one anyway."

"A couple of days is fine," I said. "Just order a new light."

Earl nodded. "And while we're waiting for that to arrive, I'll get the bodywork fixed." He looked at me closely. "Say, ain't you that supernatural investigator fella from town?"

"Yeah," I said. "I am." I had no idea how he'd recognized me. Maybe there were so few new people in Dearmont that he was able to guess who I must be.

"I saw your picture in the paper," he said.

"The paper?"

"Yeah, it was in yesterday's *Observer*. There's an article in there with a picture of both of you. How else did you think I recognized you? I'm not psychic, I leave that to June. She has a touch of psychic power now and then."

"It's a gift," June said. "I sometimes do tarot readings for the ladies at the hair salon. I told Mary Lou Robinson that her husband was going to be in an accident and two weeks later, he'd left her for another woman. Isn't that uncanny?"

I wasn't sure how she equated being in an accident with being unfaithful so I just shrugged. "Anyway, I need to be somewhere, so if I leave the Land Rover here, will you call me when it's ready to be collected? My number's on here." I handed her one of my business cards.

"Of course," she said, taking the card and reading it.

"And we'll give you a loaner while you're waiting," Earl said. "You'll need a car for your supernatural investigations and such."

"Sure," I said. I wasn't going to turn down the offer of another vehicle. It meant I wouldn't have to rely on Felicity to get around. It also meant I wouldn't have to squeeze myself into the Mini.

"I'll get the keys," June said, heading for the office.

"Could I see that newspaper too?" I asked.

"Sure thing," Earl said. "We're done with it, so you can have it."

June disappeared for a few seconds and then reappeared with a set of car keys and a folded Dearmont *Observer*. She gave me the newspaper and took the keys over to a brown Chevy that was in good condition but looked at least thirty years old.

"She's a 1985 Chevy Caprice," Earl said. "She's old but she runs just fine."

June unlocked the driver's door and opened it for me.

"Thanks," I said, looking at the boxy design of the mud-colored car and wishing Earl had something cooler on his lot, like an Impala.

I got in and June handed me the keys. The interior of the car was warm and smelled of lemon thanks to an air freshener hanging from the rearview mirror. The seats were beige velour but the fabric wasn't worn at all, despite the age of the car, so I guessed June and Earl had replaced the fabric recently. The dash was upholstered in light brown vinyl and that looked like it had been recently restored too. The way June and Earl were looking at me with expectant faces, I figured this old Caprice must be their pride and joy.

"Very nice," I said.

Earl grinned. "That's the car we spent our honeymoon in. Took her on a road trip all the way to California and back in 1987."

"She's a beauty," June said, lovingly running her hand over the bodywork.

Considering what the Land Rover had been through recently, I wondered if it might be better if they loaned me a different car. I didn't want to smash up a vehicle that gave them happy memories. But I was only going to be investigating the church and the lake in the next couple of days, so I didn't anticipate any car chases or arguments with cemetery gates. I just had to make sure Polidori didn't get behind the wheel.

I tossed the Dearmont *Observer* onto the passenger seat and thanked June and Earl again before cranking the engine. It came to life with a throaty purr. The mechanic couple had probably spent the last thirty years tinkering with the engine, or maybe even replaced it with something more powerful.

I waited for Felicity to get into her Mini before following her out of the parking lot and back onto the highway. As I left the lot, I waved to June and Earl. They waved back, watching me drive their pride and joy away.

I just hoped that when I returned the car, it would be in the same condition it was in now.

CHAPTER 3

WE REACHED THE TOWNSHIP OF Clara an hour later, after coming off the highway and following narrow roads that wound through the trees. A simple wooden sign by the roadside, bearing the name CLARA painted in uneven red letters, told us we'd reached our destination.

There were six houses, three on each side of the road, and a couple of rough patches of farmland but nothing to suggest that anyone lived here. The houses looked abandoned, the farmland neglected and overgrown.

After we drove past the houses, I spotted a small hand-painted sign that read *CHURCH* over an arrow pointing down a dirt road that looked just wide enough for a car to pass.

Felicity's Mini slowed in front of me and she turned onto the dirt road. I followed, the undergrowth at the edges of the road brushing against the sides of the Caprice. Maybe Felicity's small car had some advantages after all; it was ideal for narrow roads that led to weird churches.

I had no idea if the church actually was weird or not but I already felt creeped out just from driving along the dirt road. The trees shielded the road from the sunlight, casting an oppressive gloom over everything. Ahead, I saw the church, a tall stone building covered with dark green moss. The windows were stained glass but I couldn't make out the designs from this distance.

The church seemed incongruous sitting among the trees. There was a grassy parking area but other than that, the area around the building was heavily wooded, the trees huddling so close that they formed a natural barrier.

Felicity parked in the grassy area and I brought the Caprice to a stop next to her Mini. When I got out, the air smelled earthy and damp. Silence sat over the area like a heavy blanket. No birds sang in the trees. No insects buzzed around us. The church stood in a silent, lifeless world.

Felicity closed her car door softly, the sound of the latch clicking amplified in the quietness of the clearing, and looked around. She hugged herself as if she were cold. "This place give me the creeps, Alec."

"Yeah, me too," I said. I opened the Mini's trunk and took out an enchanted dagger in a leather sheath. I attached the sheath to my belt and then took the crystal shard pouch out of my pocket. As soon as I opened the pouch, the blue glow from inside was unmistakable. I removed the glowing crystal and held it up. "Plenty of magical energy here," I told Felicity.

I walked closer to the building. The glow's intensity increased. When I got to the church doors, I put the crystal back into its pouch and then into my jeans pocket. It had told me everything I needed to know to continue; the massacre that had occurred here was linked to supernatural forces.

Felicity stayed close behind me, her hand on my shoulder, her dark eyes wide as she looked past me to the closed church doors. "This is really spooky," she whispered into my ear.

"Yeah, it is," I agreed. I reached for the handle on the double doors and tried it. The doors were unlocked. They swung inward with a groan. The air that rushed out from the building smelled fetid and damp.

The interior of the church was lit only by sunlight filtering through four stained glass windows, throwing colorful shapes across the floor and walls. Amy had said the windows had been covered in blood when the bodies were found and there were still pale red patches on the glass.

There were old style wooden church pews and modern plastic chairs scattered around the room as if a tornado had touched down and thrown them against the walls. Most of the chairs and pews were broken.

I stepped inside, Felicity still hanging on to my shoulder. Despite the stained glass lighting effect, the interior of the church was gloomy. Shadows clung to the walls and spread over the corners. I took the Maglite from my pocket and played the light over the room. I didn't want any nasty surprises to come rushing out of those dark corners.

A slight burning sensation on my left pectoral muscle told me that one of my protective tattoos had been activated. The tattoo in that location was an eye of Horus and had been magically enchanted to allow me to see through a glamour or veiling spell. Something in this room was disguised by magic.

Thanks to the tattoo, I would see the disguised item in its true form. To the police and FBI, the item would have appeared as something else entirely when they searched the church.

"What do you see?" I asked Felicity. She would see the item in its disguised form, so if I could figure out what I was seeing differently than her with my enhanced sight, I'd know what was being hidden by the magical veil.

Where the sunlight illuminated patches of the walls, bloodstains were visible, some of them up near the ceiling. It looked like the victims of the massacre had been thrown around in the same manner as the chairs.

"Just a lot of broken furniture," she said. "And blood on the walls."

We moved forward slowly, stepping over broken chairs and splintered wood. I realized I was trying to move as quietly as possible, as if making a sound might awaken something evil that was sleeping in the building's foundations. At the far end of the church, a gray stone altar sat atop a raised dais. A wooden lectern lay next to the altar, broken in two.

I glanced up at the nearest window. The image depicted by the colored glass wasn't the usual biblical scene; it showed a cliff edge and a tempestuous sea below. On the cliff, hooded figures in white robes were performing some sort of ceremony around a magic circle. A naked woman walked calmly toward the edge of the cliff, her eyes vacant, her face devoid of emotion. I looked closer at the sea in the image. There was something dark lurking beneath the waves, waiting to rise from the depths.

"You don't see that in most churches," I whispered.

Felicity looked up at the window and frowned in confusion. ""What do you mean? The stained glass?"

"No, I mean the image."

"The crucifixion is one of the most common images in church windows, Alec."

I looked back at the window and the image of the woman walking toward the cliff edge. "The crucifixion," I said. "Right." I took out my phone and took a photo of the window. The photo showed the woman, the cliff, and the robed figures. I showed the screen to Felicity. "What do you see?"

She looked at me with narrowed eyes as if I were playing a joke on her. "You can see it for yourself, Alec. There's Christ on the cross, the Roman soldier with the spear, and Mary Magdalene at the foot of the cross." She pointed to areas of the phone screen where I saw the sea, the cliff, and the woman.

At least now I knew it was the windows that were hiding under a glamor.

"There's a spell on the windows," I told Felicity. I see something different than you because one of my tattoos is letting me see through the spell.

Her dark eyes widened. "What do you see?"

"I'll show you later. I have something at the office that will let you see past the glamor in the photos," I said.

She nodded and looked back at the window, which to her sight was nothing more than the depiction of a biblical scene. "Why would someone cast a spell on the church?"

"I don't know," I said, stepping over the debris to the next window. This one showed a beach scene. On the sand, thirteen white-robed figures dead. There were tracks on the sand as if something huge had slithered across the beach and into the sea. The water was disturbed, implying that something big had entered it and sunk beneath the surface a moment ago.

"There are thirteen dead people in that window," I told Felicity. "Thirteen victims, just like in the massacre here."

She sighed. "So you don't see John the Baptist and his followers."

35

I took a photo of the window.

The window closest to us on the opposite wall showed the resurrection of Lazarus according to Felicity. What I saw there was something very different.

The image was of a forest at night. A clearing in the distance was lit by a fire and thirteen figures danced around its perimeter. In the darkness between the trees, a pair of huge eyes glowed, watching the dancers with a malevolence that made my insides feel like they were knotting up. I wanted to flee the church, to get away from the oppressive atmosphere I suddenly felt all around me.

I was sure Felicity felt the same fear, even though she couldn't see the eyes in the window. She was breathing hard and fast in my ear, as if trying to control a panic attack. "We should get out of here, Alec."

"Just take a deep breath and try to stay calm," I said, putting my hand on hers. "There's a residue of terror in the atmosphere here and it's affecting us, that's all. There's nothing to be afraid of." But even as I said that, my eyes were scanning the dark corners of the church, expecting to see a monster lurking in the shadows. I took out my phone and took a picture of the forest image before moving to the final window.

"Mary holding baby Jesus," Felicity said before I even asked her what she saw. She obviously wanted to get this over with as soon as possible and get out of here. I felt exactly the same but we had to search this place if we were to have any chance of finding out what happened here on Christmas Day.

The stained glass image was made up of mostly red and black glass because the picture showed the interior of a cave with a blood-covered floor littered with bones and skulls. The far end of the cave was hidden in blackness and the same pair of eyes from the forest picture lurked there. I took a photo and pocketed my phone, making a conscious effort to breathe deeply. If there was some type of terror-inducing magic attached to the windows, my tattoos were helpless against it.

"Let's see what's through there," I said, pointing the Maglite beam at a closed door beside the altar.

We made our way over there, stepping over bits and pieces of broken furniture. The door was unlocked. I pushed it open to reveal a room that seemed to have served as an office. There was a single plain window that looked out over the woods at the back of the church. The dim light coming in through the window was sufficient to see by.

A large mahogany desk sat at the far end of the room. There was a computer power cable plugged into an outlet on the wall, but no computer. The FBI must have taken it as part of their investigation. A bookshelf running along one wall was empty A filing cabinet near the window was open, the top drawer empty. I had no doubt the other drawers had been cleared out too.

"What are we hoping to find?" Felicity asked. "The FBI have already been here and taken everything."

"The FBI thinks this was a mundane case. They only took things of interest to a normal murder investigation. They would have missed anything that pointed to the supernatural. Unless they sent a real-life Mulder and Scully in here, we should be able to find something of interest, because we're looking at this from a totally different angle. We just need to find what the FBI overlooked."

"But this room is empty and there's nothing in the main part of the church except broken chairs and pews."

"And those creepy windows." I cast a cursory glance around the empty office. Felicity was right; if there had ever been anything of interest here, it was gone now, probably locked away in a federal building in Boston. We needed to search in the main part of the church again if we were going to find any clues.

When we stepped back into the main room, I said to Felicity, "You check up around the altar and I'll look through the broken chairs and stuff."

"What are we looking for?" she asked.

"Anything strange. A symbol maybe, or an inscription in the walls or on the floor. It might help us to pinpoint exactly what type of magic was used here."

She went up the steps of the dais and began looking at the floor around the altar. As soon as she stepped away from me, I missed her closeness. Sure, her close proximity had been prompted by fear but it was nice all the same. I looked at the debris on the floor and sighed. Looking through this stuff was going to be like looking for a needle in a haystack.

I went over to a broken chair and lifted it up to look at the stone floor beneath.

"Alec, wait!"

I turned to face Felicity. "What is it?"

She held up a hand, telling me to wait, and climbed up onto the stone altar. When she was standing on top of it, she pointed at the mess of broken chairs and pews. "You need to see this."

I looked at the place on the floor where she was pointing. "What is it? I don't see anything."

She shook her head excitedly. "No, you have to be up here to see it."

I went up the steps of the dais and looked at the debris. From this vantage point, the mess didn't look so chaotic. I could see definite lines and curves formed by the broken furniture.

"Up here," Felicity said, beckoning me up onto the altar.

I climbed up next to her and looked at the floor of the church. The plastic chairs, metal chair legs and pieces of wood from the pews hadn't been thrown around at random at all. They formed a perfect circle and half a dozen magical glyphs, within the circle and outside of it.

Standing on the floor among the debris, the circle and magical patterns were impossible to see. The patterns could only be distinguished from up here, looking down at them from above.

"Do you recognize any of those symbols?" I asked Felicity. None of them were familiar to me, so my method of determining their identity would be to take pictures and look them up later in the Society database.

But Felicity specialized in ancient languages and occult symbols so she might know what they were just by looking at them.

"I recognize them," she said. "They belong to a language that has unknown origins. It's appeared on artifacts from ancient Egypt, ancient Rome, and even further back in history. Those artifacts are always magical or religious in nature, usually connected with evil gods or dark magic."

"So do you know what this circle represents? What those particular symbols mean?"

She narrowed her eyes and looked at the pattern with an intense stare. "I understand what some of it means. Two of the symbols are in a position relative to each other on the circle which means, 'the tearing of the veil'. I can't interpret the others without referring to some texts on the subject."

"Okay, we'll get photos of everything and examine them back at the office." I got my phone out of my pocket again and began taking pictures of the patterns on the floor. Felicity did the same with her own phone.

"I think we've seen enough," I said when we'd taken pictures of every square inch of the church floor, both with and without flash. "Let's get out of here."

"That's the best idea you've had all day," she said.

We went outside and closed the doors behind us. Even though this area of the woods was creepily silent, being outside was a thousand times better than being in the church. Even the earthy air tasted fresh as I breathed it in.

We got in the cars and I followed Felicity's Mini along the dirt road. When we reached the half dozen houses known as Clara, I saw a gray-haired woman standing among the weeds in one of the overgrown lawns. She wore a pale yellow dress that fluttered in the breeze around her thin legs. As I drove past, she fixed her pale eyes on me and scowled. I could feel the malevolence of her stare as if it were slithering into the car through the windshield.

Even when the houses were in my rearview mirror, the woman in the yellow dress was still standing at the roadside, staring after me. Then we turned a corner, Clara was lost behind the trees, and I let out a sigh of relief.

I pulled my phone out of my pocket and placed it on top of the folded copy of the Dearmont *Observer* on the passenger seat. After pressing the speaker button, I called Felicity. She answered immediately. Unlike me, she had her phone connected to her car's hands-free system.

"Let's stop at the parking lot that overlooks the lake," I said. "I'll buy you a coffee from that place there. The Coffee Hut."

"The Coffee Shack," she corrected me. "And I'll have tea."

"Of course you will. We can sit in the car and go over the Deirdre Summers case file. Maybe I'll get a better feel for the case if I can see the lake where she disappeared."

"All right," Felicity said with a teasing note in her voice. "Your car or mine?"

"Mine," I said. "There's more room in here than there is in your Mini."

"I look forward to it," she said, and ended the call.

When we reached the turnoff for Dearmont Lake, Felicity took it and I followed her to a large parking lot. We parked the cars so they faced the calm expanse of water and I got out of the Caprice while Felicity came over with the Deirdre Summers case file in her hand.

"I'll be back in a moment," I said, heading for the dark brown wooden building that was the Coffee Shack. When I got back to the Caprice with the hot drinks, Felicity was sitting in the passenger seat with her window rolled all the way down and the Dearmont *Observer* open on her lap. I got into the driver's seat and handed her a cup of tea.

"Anything interesting in there?" I asked, nodding at the newspaper.

She showed me the page she'd been reading. There was a photograph of us standing in North Cemetery with Dennis Jackson, the cemetery manager. The headline read, *WHAT IS HAPPENING IN OUR CEMETERY? ALEC*

HARBINGER, PRETERNATURAL INVESTIGATOR, IS ON THE CASE.

Wesley Jones must have taken the picture when we'd met him at the cemetery after three people, including his father, had crawled out of their graves. It had turned out to be a residual magical leak from the Box of Midnight that had caused the animation of the corpses, and we had sorted it out but the article in the *Observer* gave the impression that I was working an ongoing case at the cemetery.

Jones said that he had "stumbled upon it" while visiting his father's grave. He mentioned the disturbed earth and my reluctance to answer his questions. He said he had no idea what I was up to but noted that I'd been inspecting the graves in the cemetery closely.

Apparently, he later visited Dennis Jackson and asked for an interview on the subject but the cemetery manager's response had been, "No comment". I smiled when I read that. Dennis Jackson was good people.

The article wasn't too much of a problem. The cemetery angle was false but it would make the people of Dearmont aware that there was a P.I. in town if they needed my services. But Jones had written something at the end of the piece that made me less happy. "Alec Harbinger has a list of clients that includes Deputy Amy Cantrell of the Sheriff's Department."

I jabbed the paper with my finger. "What the hell? Has this guy been watching our office to see who comes and goes?"

"It sounds like it," Felicity said. She closed the *Observer* and refolded it before placing it on the dashboard.

"This is all we need, a nosy reporter watching our every move." I sat back in my seat and took a sip of hot coffee, watching the boats out on the lake in an effort to calm myself. It didn't work.

"What if he followed us to Clara and writes in the next issue that we're investigating the church? Not only will Sheriff Cantrell be even more pissed at me than he already is, the story could tip off our enemies. There might be some black magic sorcerer out there who thinks he got away with the Christmas Day Massacre and he'll read that I'm now on the case. That could be dangerous for the entire town if he comes gunning for me."

"I'm sure Wesley Jones didn't follow us to the church," Felicity said. "He said he owns the game store in town. Surely he'll be at work. He can't devote all his time to following you around if he has a store to run."

Her common sense calmed me a little. Still, it might be a good idea to pay Wesley Jones a visit sometime and warn him that poking his nose into my business wasn't the healthiest of options. I wasn't going to threaten him exactly but...okay, yeah, I was going to threaten him.

I picked up the Deirdre Summers file and flicked through it. There wasn't much in there. With no body, and no evidence of foul play, the police didn't have much to go on. The file contained interviews with Deirdre's friends, family, and acquaintances and some photos of the interior of her house. I guessed that Cantrell and his deputies had gone there to find Deirdre and, when they got no response from knocking on her door, forced their way inside.

I passed the interviews to Felicity and inspected the photos. Deirdre's house looked clean and tidy, the furniture neatly arranged and seemingly in its usual place. There was no indication of a struggle that might have suggested the librarian had been abducted from her home and taken forcibly to the lake.

It was when I got to the photos of Deirdre's bedroom that I knew what the sheriff and Amy had meant when they'd said there might be a preternatural element to Deirdre's disappearance.

The bedroom was in the same neat state as the other rooms except for the wall above the bed. There were maybe fifty sheets of paper pinned to the wall. In contrast to the rest of the house, the arrangement of papers was chaotic. Some were hanging on their own on the pale green bedroom wall. Others huddled together, their edges overlapping.

There were drawings on the pieces of paper, scribblings in dark pencil. The photograph I was looking at was a view of the bedroom from the doorway so the drawings were nothing more than indistinguishable dark shapes. I turned the page and discovered that the photographer had obligingly moved closer to the wall and taken close-ups of Deirdre's homemade wallpaper.

The drawings were crude but good enough that I recognized Dearmont Lake in some of them. The lake was drawn from a place that overlooked a rocky part of the shoreline, the lake stretching across the paper in the background. The small island was visible but it was no more than a dark smudge in the distance.

The rest of the drawings were of a creature emerging from the water. Deirdre was definitely no artist and the creature's form was indistinguishable from the dark shading that had been used to represent the lake but I could see a pair of bulbous eyes and a frog-like mouth.

I passed the file to Felicity. "What do you think of this?"

She laid the file on her lap and pursed her lips as she examined the drawings. "Do you think there's a connection between these drawings and what you saw on the windows in the church?"

"I think it's likely. The windows showed something being summoned from water and Deirdre's drawings are similar. But the drawings are more specific about the location. They show this lake."

I looked out at the water shimmering in the sun. Did something lurk in the depths beneath the fishing boats and pleasure craft? Had Deirdre Summers somehow seen the monster that was hinted at in the stained glass windows of the church at Clara?

"I think there's probably a connection between the two cases," I told Felicity. "It might be tenuous, considering Deirdre drew those pictures three years ago and the church massacre took place on Christmas Day last year, but we should keep an open mind."

She pointed at the drawing of the creature rising from the water. "Do you think this thing actually exists or is it a figment of Deirdre Summers' imagination?"

"Whatever killed those people at the church wasn't imaginary. Whether or not it was the creature in the drawings and the windows is something we have to find out."

I took out my phone and flicked through the photos of the stained glass windows. The eyes in the dark woods and the suggestion of a huge shape lurking beneath the water made me shudder.

Just looking at images that suggested this thing existed made the hairs on the back of my neck stand up.

So how the hell was I supposed to destroy it?

CHAPTER 4

WHEN WE GOT BACK TO the office, I told Felicity to go ahead inside and that I'd be there soon. I walked down Main Street beneath the blazing midday sun until I reached a store called Dearmont Games. In the window, there was a display of tabletop RPG games, metal miniatures of knights and wizards, and various dice and card games.

I went inside, feeling the store's AC cool the sweat on my forehead. It was a hot day for monster hunting but at least I had a cool environment in which to warn Wesley Jones away from my business.

The interior of the store was racked out with metal shelving crammed with brightly-colored game boxes, paperback fantasy books, and action figures of fantasy and science fiction characters. Inside a glass-topped display case in the center of the store, two armies of metal miniatures faced each other across a battlefield of fake grass and plastic ruins.

The counter was a long glass cabinet that displayed more figurines, games, and dice. Standing behind it, his nose buried in a Warhammer paperback, was Timothy Ellsworth, a young man who had recently become a werewolf and asked for my help in keeping him restrained during the full moon.

"Hey, Timothy," I said.

He looked up from the book and his face brightened. "Alec! How are you?" Then he frowned and lowered his voice to a whisper. "What are you doing here? It isn't the full moon yet."

"No, I'm not here for that," I said, taking his cue to drop my voice to a whisper even though there were no customers in the store. "I came to see Wesley Jones. Is he here?"

He hesitated. "Ummm…"

"I know he's here," I told him.

Timothy's eyes widened. "How do you know that? Some sort of magic?"

I grinned and shook my head. "If nobody else is here, then why are we whispering?"

He let out a sigh and pointed to a door at the rear of the store marked Staff Only. "He's in the alley having a smoke. He sits on the dumpster out there. He told me that if you came by, I was to tell you he wasn't here."

So, Wesley had guessed that I'd be paying him a visit after reading his article and now he was in hiding. In a small town like this, how long did he hope to avoid me?

"I was going to tell you he was here, even if you hadn't deduced it," Timothy said. "You're my friend, Alec, and I trust you with my biggest secret."

"Speaking of which," I said as I walked toward the rear door, "just make sure your boss never finds out or it'll be all over the Dearmont *Observer*."

"I know that," he said, giving me a little wave as I opened the door and went out into the alley.

Wesley was sitting on a blue dumpster smoking a cigarette. When he saw me come out of his store and walk toward him, his mouth dropped open and the cigarette fell to the ground, where it sparked for a brief second before dying.

Wesley followed it, sliding off the dumpster with an agility borne of fear, and I thought he was going to run but he stumbled backward and found himself trapped between the dumpster and me. "Before you say anything, the people of Dearmont have a right to know what's happening in their town," he said, his eyes wide with fear behind his glasses.

"You've been spying on me, Wesley," I said calmly. I was angry but there was no need to shout. Sometimes, cool detachment is scarier.

"Not spying. I just happened to be at the cemetery at the same time as you and I put two and two together."

"And came up with five," I said. "There's no problem at the cemetery. I'm not investigating anything there."

"Even after what happened last night?" he asked.

"What happened last night?" I gave nothing away, unsure of how much he knew about the zombies on Main Street. There hadn't been many witnesses.

Wesley shrugged. "I'm not exactly sure and nobody will officially talk to me about it but there were rumors flying around town this morning that some residents of the old South Cemetery were seen walking through town. That must be connected to you, am I right?"

I said nothing.

"Would you give me an exclusive interview?" he asked hopefully.

"Don't push it, Wesley."

"Okay, fine. But I haven't been spying on you, I swear. I'm just observant."

"So that's how you knew Amy Cantrell had been to my office? Because you were being observant?"

"I can see your office from my store window," he said. "I don't even have to go out onto the sidewalk. I saw the deputy go to your place and then I ran into you at the cemetery. It was coincidence. I swear it. My spying days are over now."

I moved closer to him. He was a small guy and I towered over him. He shrank back slightly but the dumpster prevented him from escaping. If it wasn't there,

51

I was sure he would have fled by now. "What do you mean they're over now? So you were spying on me before?"

He shook his head so vigorously that his glasses were in danger of flying off his face. "No, no, not you. I never spied on you."

"Who then?"

He swallowed and looked down at the ground nervously.

"Who were you spying on, Wesley?"

He looked up at me with pleading eyes. "It was a long time ago. Last year. It doesn't matter now."

I also put two and two together but, unlike Wesley, I was pretty sure I'd come up with the correct answer. His interest in my work and close proximity to my office made it obvious who he'd been spying on last year. "Sherry Westlake," I said.

His eyes went even wider and he looked up and down the alley as if expecting my predecessor to be standing there. "Don't tell her," he said. "Please."

"How the hell would I tell her? Sherry Westlake disappeared on Christmas Day."

"I know that. But you P.I.s are tight, aren't you? And you all work for the same parent company or something, right? I mean, if anyone knows where she is, it will be you. Am I right?"

"You're wrong. I have no idea where she is, or even if she's still alive."

"Okay," he said, breathing a sigh of relief. "That's good."

"You seem pretty scared of her," I said.

"Yeah, well, she had her suspicions that I might be watching her and she told me, in no uncertain terms, to keep away from her." He rubbed his throat and said, "She pinned me against a wall and held a knife to my throat."

Way to go, Sherry, I thought. "It sounds like you deserved it, Wesley."

He shrugged. "I was only taking a few photos and following her around now and then. This town is too quiet to make a living as a reporter. Sure, I have the store but journalism is my true passion. And the only way to get any good stories is to follow you guys around. You always know where the action is."

"But you didn't get any stories from following Sherry," I told him. "I read your articles online. You never wrote about her."

"I was going to publish a big story," he said. "An investigation into the life of a preternatural investigator. I was going to ask some hard-hitting questions too, like who are the P.I.s, what company do they work for, and are they needed in a society where nobody believes in the supernatural anymore. It was going to be a great piece and it might have made my name known to some of the big-hitters like the *Boston Globe* or even *the New York Times*."

"But you didn't publish it," I said.

He shook his head. "I couldn't, could I? While I was writing it and...observing...Sherry Westlake, that church thing happened and the feds were suddenly crawling over everything to do with her. They came to town asking questions, wanting to know who had hired her, who visited her office, that kind of thing. When they went to search her office, the place was empty, cleaned out like she'd never been there at all. The feds were fuming over that."

I nodded. The Society would have cleaned the place to prevent Sherry's notes and computer falling into the wrong hands. "So you were following Sherry just before she disappeared. Did the FBI take your photos and research?"

"No way, I never told them anything. I didn't want them to think I was involved in any way. That might make me a suspect."

I considered the implications of what he'd just told me. If he'd been spying on Sherry Westlake just before the church massacre, his photos and records of her movements might contain a clue about what happened in Clara. Sherry must have had some knowledge about the church to be investigating it in the first place. If I looked at Wesley's material, maybe I could pick up on something second-hand.

"Here's what's going to happen," I told him. "You're going to box up everything you have on Sherry Westlake and you're going to deliver it to my office. Then I'll forget about you sticking your nose into my business at the cemetery and everyone will be happy."

He swallowed and nodded. "Okay, I can do that. When do you want me to bring the stuff over?"

"Today. Leave it with my assistant because I don't think I want to see your face again for a while. Understood?"

"Of course. Can I get back to the store now?"

I stepped back slightly to give him room to get past me. "You can but remember that I want that material today. Don't make me come back here tomorrow."

"You'll get it today," he promised, scurrying to the door.

"One other thing," I said, stopping him in his tracks.

He looked at me expectantly.

"Timothy didn't tell me you were out here," I said. "I found out by magic."

"Okay," he said.

I raised an eyebrow at him as if to say, "Why are you still here?" He opened the door and disappeared inside.

After he was gone, I stood in the alley, feeling a hot tingling sensation rise from the base of my spine, up to my shoulders, and down along my arms. I'd only felt it once before, when I'd sent a lethal blast of magical energy at DuMont in the cemetery.

What I felt now wasn't as strong and it didn't feel like it was going to escape my body unless I let it. I had the feeling that if I stood still and breathed deeply a few times, the tingling would pass and the energy I felt in my hands would dissipate.

But what would that prove? Something had been unlocked within me when I'd touched the statue of Hapi at the British Museum and I needed to know what it was. Controlling it and making it go away wouldn't get me any closer to understanding what it was.

I checked that I was alone in the alley and stepped back from the blue dumpster, deciding it would be as good a target as any. I flung my arms forward, palms facing the dumpster, and willed the energy to leave my body.

The air in front of my hands crackled with bright green energy that formed itself into an intricate circle and glyph combination before becoming a streak of blinding green light that shot forward and hit the dumpster.

I expected the dumpster to maybe crumple a little where it was hit but the force of the blast sent it tumbling end over end down the alley. The metal slammed onto the ground each time the dumpster touched down, the sound thundering off the walls of the surrounding buildings.

After four revolutions, the dumpster skidded to a halt, upside-down and about thirty feet from its original location.

I needed to get back to the office because if this was anything like the last time I'd fired a bolt of energy, I would soon lose all my strength. As I passed the door to the game store, it opened and Timothy poked his head out to see what the noise was.

"Alec?" he asked. "What happened?"

"Your boss is going to have to find a new place to smoke," I said as I walked out of the alley.

CHAPTER 5

I FELT FINE WHEN I got to the office but I remembered that after blasting DuMont, I'd had time to drive Mallory home and have a conversation with her before collapsing on the lawn. As I passed Felicity's office, I stuck my head through the doorway, told her about my encounter with Wesley Jones, and said that he would be coming over later with the Sherry Westlake material.

"No problem," she said.

"I'm going to go into my office for a while," I said.

"You said you had something here that would let me see those windows the same way you saw them. Can I have a look at the photos now?"

"Sure, I don't see why not." Actually, I could think of a lot of reasons why not, one of them being that I might collapse from exhaustion at any time, but I felt good at the moment and I wanted Felicity to see the windows in their true form. I particularly wanted her to see the magic circle in the cliff scene because she might recognize it and bring us one step closer to discovering the type of magic that had been practiced at the church.

She followed me into my office and I put my phone on the desk before rummaging in one of the drawers for something I had put in there along with numerous other small magical items. I found it at the back of the drawer and laid it on the desk next to the phone.

Felicity recognized the flat round stone with a hole in its center. "A faerie stone," she said. "I've heard about those. People used to use them to see faeries."

"That's right," I said. "Looking through the hole in the center of the stone allows you to see through magical veils and glamors." Switching on my phone, I found a photo of the first window, the one with the ritual on the cliff and the woman walking toward the sea. "Take a look," I said to Felicity.

She picked up the pale gray stone and removed her glasses, setting them down on my desk. Her dark eyes looked expectant. She loved things like this, seeing beyond the normal into a world beyond. Her study of languages and magical symbols was all about looking beyond the mundane world and finding something more.

She held the faerie stone up to her right eye.

"Try the left eye," I told her. "According to the folklore, the left eye is better at seeing otherworldly things."

She switched the stone to her left eye and looked down at my phone through the hole in the stone's center. When she gasped and stepped back slightly, I knew she'd seen beyond the glamor spell to the image that was actually on the window.

"That's horrible," she said.

"Do you see the magic circle?"

"Yes, but I don't recognize it at the moment. I'll try to find out what exactly it is."

I flicked to a photo of the next window, the one with the dead robed figures on the beach.

"Creepy," Felicity said.

I showed her the photo of the fire and the dancers in the woods. When she saw it, a look of revulsion crossed Felicity's face. "Oh, my God, what is that in the trees? I can only see its eyes but that's enough to scare me."

She lowered the stone and looked away, her eyes moving to the window and the clear blue sky beyond. "I don't like this, Alec."

"Me neither," I admitted. "I don't know if the windows have been enchanted with some sort of terror spell or if the creature in those pictures is so bad that it causes a fear response."

"It's horrible." She looked down at my phone again and put the faerie stone to her eyes. "All right, show me the last one."

I found a photo of the bloody cave littered with bones and the eyes in the darkness. Felicity looked at it for a moment and then put the stone down. "I've seen enough. Basically, we're dealing with a bloody scary monster."

"Yeah, looks like it." I felt a sudden weakness in my legs and leaned against the desk. But as I did so, my arms became weak too and couldn't support my weight. "Shit," I murmured as I felt myself sinking to the floor. I tried to grab my chair but it rolled away and I went down, ending up on my back on the carpet.

"Alec!" Felicity rushed around the desk and knelt by me, her face worried. "Should I get an ambulance?"

"No," I said weakly. "I'll be fine in a minute. Help me get into the chair." If I was going to spend a few minutes recovering, I'd rather do it sitting in my chair than lying on the floor.

She nodded and put her arms under mine, helping me get to my knees before rolling the chair over to me. "Ready?" she asked. "On the count of three. One. Two. Three." She heaved with all her strength and I pushed against the floor with legs that felt like strings of overcooked spaghetti.

When I was in the chair, I said, "Thanks," and sat there for a moment looking at the ceiling. This wasn't as bad as when I'd been helpless on the lawn after blasting DuMont and I was sure I'd be okay in a couple of minutes.

When I moved my gaze from the ceiling back to my desk, Felicity was sitting across from me in one of the client chairs, her glasses back on her face and a look that was a mix of concern and anger in her eyes. "Are you going to tell me what's going on?" she asked.

I sighed. She had a right to know. "Okay, but this is between you and me. I don't want anyone else finding out about it, especially not the Society."

Felicity nodded. "Of course. You know you can trust me."

She was right, I did. "When I was fighting DuMont in the old cemetery, something weird happened. After Mallory destroyed the heart inside the Box of Midnight and took Rekhmire's curse into herself, I was so angry and upset that I felt my emotions rising like a ball of energy inside me. Some sort of magical power entered my hands and I directed it at DuMont. It killed him. Later that night, after Mallory left, I collapsed on to the lawn, which was where you found me."

"And now you've collapsed again," she said. "This isn't good, Alec. What if it's slowly draining you? What if…"

I held up a weak hand to stop her. "This isn't the result of the same blast. I used the magic again earlier on a dumpster."

"Well that was foolish," she chided.

"Yes, it probably was. But I need to know what's happening to me and the only way I can do that is to experiment."

"And then later collapse? No, that isn't a good plan. You could kill yourself."

"How else am I going to know what's happening?" I asked.

"We can study it, find out where it comes from. In controlled conditions. And why not tell the Society? They're experts in this kind of thing. They have people who can…"

"No," I said. "The Society is going through a close examination by the witches who run it in an attempt to flush out traitors belonging to a rival group. I'm not going to reveal this to anyone there. Besides, my father already knows about it."

"You told him?"

"No, he's somehow involved with taking away my memories of it. When I went to the British Museum, I thought the only memories I'd lost were the ones about Paris, the ones the *satori* took from me. But after I performed the ritual with the statue, it turned out that those were only minor. When the door in my mind was unlocked, I recovered some deeper, older memories of my childhood."

All of my strength had returned now. I stretched and flexed my muscles, testing them out. Good as new.

"When I was a kid," I told Felicity, "I used the magical blast on a bully. That memory was locked away, along with the memory of my mother's death."

She frowned. "But your mother died in a car crash while you were at your aunt's house. You remembered that before. You told me about it."

"That was a false memory. I was actually in the car with my mother and we were attacked. She told me to run for the trees and not look back. I did as she asked. She was murdered."

Felicity looked shocked. "I'm so sorry, Alec."

"There's something else I remember now too. When I was still a child, my father took me to the Coven, the nine witches that formed the Society, and had them perform some sort of ritual on me so that I'd forget the magic I'd used on the bully and also to put a false memory of my mother's death into my head."

Her eyes went wide. "Do you think he knows about your mother's murder? Do you think he's trying to cover something up?"

I shook my head. "My father believes the story that my mother was killed in a car accident. He has no idea what really happened. I'm probably the only person who knows that she was murdered."

"You and the people who murdered her," she added.

"Yeah. I think my father took me to the Coven to wipe my memory of the magic inside me and the witches accidentally took the memory of the night my mother died too. Or maybe they did it on purpose. I don't know."

Felicity shook her head slowly, her mind obviously trying to take in what I'd just told her. "But why would your father tell them to take away your memory of the magic?"

"I don't know. But he probably panicked after I came back from Paris because he knew the *satori* had been altering my memories. She might have opened that door in my mind by mistake. That's probably why he sent you here to spy on me, to see if my memory of using the magic during my childhood returned.

"As it turned out, the *satori* didn't touch the magical door in my mind, even though she knew it was there, and I got the childhood memories back as a side-effect of trying to get my Paris memories back."

Felicity nodded. "So your father doesn't know you have your magic power again."

"No, he doesn't, and that's the way I want to keep it for now."

"But you'll have to speak to him about it eventually. He probably knows what it is and where it came from."

"I was hoping we could find that out ourselves," I said. "This is the kind of thing you specialize in."

"I have to admit, I'm intrigued," she said.

"So let's keep this between us for now. Agreed?"

"All right."

The phone in her office rang and she went to answer it.

I wondered if I should go and see the Blackwell sisters. It was they who had discovered that there was a magical locked door in my mind and found out that an enchantment had been cast on me. Maybe if I went to see them now, they could tell me if the door was now open and the enchantment gone. Like going back to a doctor after having treatment.

Felicity called me from her office. I went in there and she handed the phone to me. "Sheriff Cantrell," she whispered.

"Sheriff, how can I help you?" I said into the phone.

"Have you had time to look at that case file yet?" he asked gruffly.

"I have," I said. "There isn't a lot of information in there."

"What about the drawings pinned to her wall? Don't tell me you missed those."

"No, I saw them," I assured him.

"So what do you think? Was Deirdre crazy or was there a real monster?"

"It's difficult to say from a bunch of drawings, Sheriff. I need to investigate further."

"*We* need to investigate further," he reminded me.

"Yeah, that," I said. "How about you take me to the place where her clothes were found?"

"Okay, I can do that. I'll pick you up…"

"Tomorrow," I said. "I have to prepare some stuff first. And can you bring the original drawings with you?"

He huffed. "I suppose so. Do you really need them? It's going to be a pain in the ass getting hold of them. They're locked up in…"

"I really need them," I said. I didn't feel guilty about putting Cantrell to the trouble of getting Deirdre's drawings from whatever evidence room they were locked up in. I knew he was going to be riding my ass throughout this entire investigation so I might as well put difficulties in his way whenever I could.

"Tomorrow at ten," he said. "Be at the station and ready to go."

"Will do, Sheriff," I said and hung up.

"You're working with the sheriff tomorrow?" Felicity asked.

"Looks like it. If he can show me where Deirdre was standing by the lake, I might be able to get a fix on her with some enchanted items, but it was three years ago so I'm not really hopeful."

"What if you can't pick anything up?"

I shrugged. "Then I guess I'll talk to Deirdre Summers' daughter and try to find out if her mom showed any signs of magical possession before she disappeared. Or if she was connected with the church in Clara in any way."

"Send me those photos and I'll work on trying to decipher that magic circle," she said. "I'll look at that circle made out of broken furniture too."

I sent her the photos. "Keep the faerie stone," I said. "I have a few of them."

Her face brightened. "Thank you."

"Yeah, well, consider it a 'welcome home' gift. It's good to have you back, Felicity."

"It's good to be back," she said. Then a flicker of sadness entered her eyes and she added, "Despite the way things ended up with Jason."

"Hey, don't worry about that now," I said, trying to cheer her up. "You know what? Why don't we leave here early today and go over the case at my house, with pizza and beers?"

She smiled. "Sounds good."

"As soon as Wesley Jones brings that box over, we're done here. In the meantime, I'm going to pay our witchy neighbors a visit."

"The Blackwell sisters?"

"Yeah, maybe they can tell me if the locked door in my mind is really gone. Give me a magical all-clear."

"All right. I'll start on the magic circle research." She went around the desk to her chair and sat down before tapping away on her computer keyboard.

"See you later," I said, leaving her office and heading down the stairs.

When I got outside, I squinted against the sunlight reflecting from parked cars and store windows. It was a beautiful day, there was no doubt about that.

I walked along Main Street toward Blackwell Books at an easy pace, taking in my surroundings, saying hello to

DARK MAGIC

people on the street who recognized me, and just enjoying the warm afternoon.

The thought of kicking back with Felicity later over pizzas and beer lightened my mood. Even the thought of working with Sheriff Cantrell tomorrow didn't faze me.

But when I got to the bookshop and was about to push through the door, something made me stop in my tracks. The hairs on the back of my neck bristled and I spun around, expecting to find someone standing right behind me. There was no one there.

I looked up and down the street but, apart from the townsfolk walking along the sidewalk and enjoying the day, there was nobody else around. Nothing to be concerned about.

Scanning the cars that drove along the street, I didn't see anything that would set my senses on edge.

Still watching the street, I opened the door of Blackwell Books and stepped inside, my good mood shattered.

CHAPTER 6

ALEC HARBINGER," VICTORIA BLACKWELL SAID from behind the counter as I entered the bookshop, "what a surprise!"

"Is it really?" I asked.

"Well, no, Devon did say something about you coming to visit us today. Still, it's nice to see you. To what do we owe the pleasure?"

I looked around the shop to see if we were alone, but the stacks of books and the arrangement of the shelves made it impossible to know if there were any customers here or not, so I kept my voice low. "The last time I came, your sister discovered a magical door in my head and your rune amulet detected an enchantment on me."

She nodded, her long raven hair tumbling over her shoulders. The wildness of her hair contrasted against the

Victorian black lace dress that she wore buttoned up to her chin. She could have worn that dress to any gathering in the nineteenth century and seemed like she was a part of polite society but that wild, unruly hair, untethered by pins or ribbons, would never do.

"Of course I remember. We had tea in the back room and you brought your lovely friend with you. Mallory, I believe her name was?"

I nodded, the memory of the foul herbal tea they had served making me grimace. "I'd like you and your sister to check me over again. I think I've opened the door and retrieved all of my memories but I want a second opinion."

She raised her eyebrows. "Yes, we can do that for you. There is the matter of payment, though."

"What? I already owe you a favor from last time. I'm only asking you to do one little thing."

"Yes, you owe us a favor for casting a werewolf locator spell," she said, nodding. "This is a different matter so it will require additional payment."

"Okay, so what do you want, another favor? I'll owe you two, how about that?"

She looked at me closely. "No, I don't think so. Something more immediate would be preferable."

I sighed, wondering if coming here had been a mistake. The last time I'd been here, I'd agreed to exchange a favor for the sisters casting a werewolf locator spell. I'd needed to find the werewolf in town so I could save lives. But now, being checked out magically by the sisters wasn't imperative. I could live without it. "Never mind," I said. "I changed my mind." I turned to the door.

Victoria said, "No need to be like that, Alec. Come on, we'll find Devon and check you over."

"What about the payment?" I asked.

She waved a slender hand in the air dismissively. "We'll forego the payment on this occasion. We don't want to fall out with the town's preternatural investigator, do we? Come on." She disappeared behind a stack of books.

What she'd said about falling out with the town's P.I. made me run after her. "Hey, did you ever work with the P.I. who was in town before me?"

"Sherry Westlake?" she asked, leading me through the maze of bookshelves to the back of the shop. "Yes, of course."

"What kind of things did you do for her?"

"Oh, the usual. Minor magics, locator spells, enchanting items, that sort of thing."

"Did she ever mention a church in Clara?"

Victoria stopped and turned to face me. "You mean the church where thirteen people died." It wasn't a question, and the lightness in her voice was gone to be replaced by a somber tone.

I nodded. "Yeah, that place."

"That place is evil," she said quietly.

"I know. Did Sherry ever mention it to you?"

72

"No," she said simply, turning around again and continuing toward the rear of the shop.

I followed, wondering if she knew anything else about the church. As a witch, she probably got a bad vibe in her magical senses every time the place was mentioned so maybe it was nothing more than that. Or maybe she knew more about the church and the Fairweather family who owned it than she was letting on.

"Alec, how nice to see you," came a voice from behind me. I turned to see Devon Blackwell, Victoria's younger and more psychic sister. She wore a Victorian-style dress as well, only hers was of dark red velvet. Like Victoria, Devon wore her black hair long and untethered.

"I'm sure you knew I was coming," I said.

"Well, I didn't say it was a surprise, did I?"

"No, but your sister did earlier. Maybe she doubts your power of prophecy."

Devon smiled and waggled a finger at me as if I were a naughty child. "Now there's no need for that. Come into the back room and we'll see if that door in your mind is still closed."

I followed them into the small room from which they ran the mail-order side of their business. Stacks of boxes flanked a metal desk with a computer sitting on it. An old sofa and wooden coffee table were the main features of the room. A pungent smell of herbs came from a kitchenette area where the sisters made their tea.

"Would you like a cup of tea?" Victoria asked when she saw me looking at the kitchenette.

"No, thank you," I said quickly.

"All right, take a seat," she said, indicating the sofa.

I sat and Devon joined me, taking my hands in hers and closing her eyes. Her hands were warm, her grip loose. After a couple of seconds, she whispered, "The door that was inside your mind is gone. You must have used powerful magic to remove it."

"Ancient Egyptian," I said.

Victoria shot me a glance, telling me to be quiet.

Devon began to tremble slightly and a look of fear settled on her face. "Thirteen times thirteen," she whispered.

"What does that mean?" I asked.

Victoria held up a hand. She'd told me before not to interrupt Devon when she was in one of her trances but I needed details, not vague prophecies.

Devon's eyes flew open. She looked around the room fearfully. "I don't want to look at it. I can't." Her grip on my hands tightened until she was almost crushing my fingers.

Then her eyes rolled back in her head and she repeated, "Thirteen times thirteen."

I didn't like this. Devon's trance state was creepy. I waited to see if she would say anything else, preferably to explain what thirteen times thirteen meant, but she fell silent and closed her eyes again. When she opened them again, she looked at me and said, "I don't know what it means."

Great. What point was the power of prophecy if it was so vague?

"Thanks," I said. At least I knew the magical door was gone from my head. I got up from the sofa.

Victoria put a hand on my shoulder. "Wait. Before you go, we might as well check if the enchantment is gone."

I frowned. "What do you mean? I thought the false memories were the enchantment. They're gone now. Devon just said so."

"Still, there's no harm in checking. This is magic that we're talking about. Things aren't always straightforward." She pulled the rune-engraved stone from her pocket and hung it on its leather cord near my chest. "Freyja, adept of the mysteries, open our eyes to the magic which has been hidden from our sight."

The amulet began to spin.

CHAPTER 7

THERE IS STILL AN ENCHANTMENT on you," Victoria said, watching the spinning amulet.

I wasn't so sure. "Maybe it's just picking up the enchantments on my tattoos."

Devon shook her head. "No, this is something much deeper."

I looked from Victoria to Devon. "And you can't tell me what kind of enchantment it is?"

The both shook their heads. "If we did some research," Victoria said. "May we take a lock of hair from you?"

"No, thanks, I think I'll pass."

"You don't trust us, do you?" Devon asked.

I opened the door and said, "Don't take it personally. In my line of work, suspicion is healthy and can keep you alive."

"How terrible," Victoria said. "That really is no life at all, Alec. Everyone needs friends."

"I have friends," I said, walking back into the main part of the bookshop. I navigated my way through the stacks of books until I could see the front door. The witches were right; I didn't trust them. Certainly not with a lock of my hair. But I might need to use them again in the future so I kept my mouth shut.

When I reached the door, Victoria said, "Good luck with the enchantment."

"See you again soon," Devon added.

"Yeah, right, thanks." I went out onto Main Street and walked back to the office. My good mood was not only shattered now, it was in tiny fragments. I couldn't believe there was still an enchantment on me. What the hell did it mean? Maybe the magical ability was coming from it but that didn't make much sense since I'd first used magic when I was just a kid. It seemed unlikely that an enchantment had been cast on me then but, knowing my father, I couldn't rule anything out.

By the time I pushed through the door to my office and ascended the narrow stairs, I was in a dark mood. It was in my nature to find answers to questions and solve cases. Not knowing what kind of spell had been cast on me or why annoyed me.

Felicity was in her office, at her computer. She looked up at me over the rim of her glasses and said, "Wesley

Jones was here. He brought the Sherry Westlake material over."

"Great, where is it?"

"On the floor in your office."

I opened my office door and was surprised by the size of the cardboard box sitting on the floor by my desk. I'd been expecting something the size of a shoe box but this was so tall that it came up to my waist. Wesley had sealed it with packing tape.

"How much research did he do on Sherry?" I asked. "He must have been following her for months."

"I don't think it's all papers," Felicity said. "He told me there's something else inside the box that you'll want to see."

I shrugged. "Okay." Whatever it was, it could wait until later. I might not be in the best of humor but I still wanted to go over the Westlake stuff with Felicity at my house. And I needed pizza. I'd hardly eaten today and that wasn't helping my mood at all.

Taking out my phone, I called Mallory and got her voicemail. "Hey, Mallory, it's Alec. Just wondering how you are. Call me anytime." When I ended the call, I wondered if her phone had gone to voicemail because it was turned off or if she was avoiding me and had rejected my call. I really didn't need to go there; I was feeling low enough already.

Telling myself to snap out of it, I made a second call, this time to Al's Pizzeria, and ordered a large pepperoni pizza. That made me feel a little better.

I called to Felicity, "We need to leave now. It's urgent."

She appeared at the door, a worried look on her face. "Why? What's happened?"

"We need to beat the pizza guy to my house," I said.

She let out a sigh of relief and then stood with her hands on her hips, her expression serious. "That's not funny, Alec. If I had something to throw at you right now, I'd use it."

"Well, instead of doing that, throw yourself into that tiny car of yours and let's go to my place."

"Fine, just let me switch my computer off first." She went back into her office and I heard her fussing around in there.

I picked up the box. The damn thing was heavy. "What the hell did Wesley put in here?"

"I have no idea." Felicity crossed the hall to the top of the stairs. "But it looks like I'll be getting my hands on that pizza first." She laughed and went downstairs quickly.

"Fine," I said as I followed her down, "but you'll have to pay the delivery guy."

She was already gone.

* * *

I got to my place and parked the Caprice in the driveway. The blue Mini was in the driveway next door but there was no sign of Felicity. I opened the Caprice's trunk and hauled the big cardboard box out. I'd had to squash it down to fit it inside the trunk and had felt something solid through the cardboard. I was intrigued.

I took it inside and set it down on the living room floor before going into the kitchen to make coffee. As I looked out of the kitchen window to the trees at the bottom of the yard, I got that feeling of being watched again. Despite the brightness of the day, the shadows down there were dark and impenetrable. Anyone could be hiding there, watching me through the window.

"Get a grip, Harbinger," I told myself, figuring I'd seen enough pictures of scary monsters today to set my nerves on edge. I was just being paranoid. I closed the blinds anyway.

A knock at the door turned my attention from paranoia to pizza and I went quickly to open it, finding Felicity on the front porch. "I thought you were the pizza guy," I said. "I'm disappointed."

The truth was, I wasn't disappointed at all. Felicity had changed into a black blouse that had a plunging neckline and lace around the neck and hem. She had changed her "exploring the old church" jeans for a tight black pair that showed off the curves of her thighs. And she had let her hair out of the pins that usually kept it piled up on top of her head so that it hung loosely around her neck and shoulders.

She shot me a mock incredulous look and said, "Fine, I'll go home and leave you alone with your pepperoni."

I laughed and stepped back from the door. She slipped in past me and I caught a subtle scent of perfume that smelled enticingly of lotus flower.

Closing the door, I said, "Make yourself at home. Coffee?"

"I thought we were having beer?" she said as she went into the living room and sat on the sofa, her dark eyes on the box.

"Yes," I said. "Beer." Her appearance had taken me off guard and I wondered if I should change too. I was still wearing the same clothes I'd worn in the church and they were dusty and dirty.

Grabbing two bottles of Bud from the fridge, I put them on the coffee table and said, "Help yourself. I'll be right back." I took the stairs to my bedroom two at a time and found a fresh pair of blue jeans and a black Harley Davison T-shirt.

I changed quickly and checked myself in the mirror before frowning at my own reflection. "What the hell do you think you're doing, Harbinger? This isn't a date, it's work." I was right, of course. Just because Felicity had showed up looking like a million dollars in a black denim and lace package didn't mean anything.

Besides, she was still getting over Jason. I would never be able to live with myself if I took advantage of her recent breakup and became some sort of "rebound guy".

I went back downstairs as the pizza guy knocked on the door. Felicity had been going to answer it but I beat her to it, opening the door before she reached it.

The delivery guy was a dark-haired young man in his early twenties and he wore an *Al's Pizzeria* dark green cap and T-shirt. "Twenty-four-inch pepperoni pizza," he said, handing me the large flat box he'd been holding. The smell of pepperoni and melted mozzarella drifted up through the cardboard, making my mouth water.

I paid him and gave him a tip. He smiled and said, "Thanks. Have a great evening." His eyes flickered to Felicity then back to me and he gave me a wink before turning and heading down the driveway to his car.

When I turned to face Felicity, she was smiling. "Well, that was rather cheeky of him."

"Yeah," I said, taking the pizza into the living room and putting it on the coffee table. I opened the box and the mouth-watering smells got even stronger, rising into the living room with the steam from the hot pizza.

"It's too hot to eat yet," Felicity said.

"We have plenty of time," I said, pointing at the big cardboard box on the floor. "Let's open the mystery box and see what's inside."

She nodded and began picking at the edge of the packing tape with her fingernails until she had enough free to tear the tape off the top of the box.

I opened it and looked inside. There were papers and photos in there, pinned to the bottom of the box by a large stone disc. I reached in and pulled it out, putting it on the floor because there was no more room on the coffee table.

"What's that?" Felicity asked.

The stone disc was the size of a Frisbee and had a hole in its center like a faerie stone. But inserted into the hole was a piece of white crystal. The dark surface of the stone had symbols and lines painted onto it in white paint. All the lines radiated from the center circle.

"It's called an Apollo Stone," I said. "Investigators use them to find out what's happening in a particular area while they're not around. Like a recording device."

She frowned. "Wouldn't a camera be better?"

"The Apollo Stone is different than a camera. It doesn't need a battery because it's charged by sunlight hitting the crystal. It doesn't need to be pointed in any specific direction because it records the entire area around it. The range depends on the size of the stone disc. This one would have a range of maybe fifty or sixty feet. And unlike a camera, the Apollo Stone ignores mundane activity and only picks up events that are connected to magic or the supernatural."

Felicity nodded. "So why did Wesley Jones have this and where did it come from?"

I shrugged, tipping out the contents of the box onto the floor. Loose papers, notebooks, and photographs slid across the carpet. Felicity got down onto the floor and examined some of the papers. "If there's anything here that explains why Wesley had an Apollo Stone, it'll take ages to find it."

"There's an easier way," I said, looking up the number for Dearmont Games on my phone. When I found it, I called the store.

My call was answered immediately. "Dearmont Games, Wesley speaking, how can I help you?"

"It's Alec Harbinger," I said.

"So you want to know about the stone," he said. "Do you know what it is?"

"Yeah, I want to know how and where you got it. I'm assuming you saw Sherry Westlake leave it somewhere and then you went and picked it up."

"Not right away," he said. "I didn't go get it until after she disappeared. I figured she wouldn't be coming back for it, with the feds searching for her and all. So I kept it with the other stuff. I've poked and prodded it and tried to look it up on the internet but I don't know what it is or what it does."

"When and where did you see her put it?" I asked him. "And when did you go get it?"

"Let's see," he said, "I saw her hide it in some bushes maybe a week before Christmas. I collected it on New

Year's Day, a week after Westlake disappeared. So what the hell is it? Is it important?"

"I don't know. You haven't told me where Sherry hid it."

"Oh, right. It was on the island. Whitefish Island in the middle of the lake."

CHAPTER 8

"SHERRY HAD MADE A CONNECTION between the church and the lake," I told Felicity after ending the call with Wesley. "While she was investigating the church, she put the Apollo Stone on the island in the middle of the lake. Whitefish Island. Wesley watched her from the docks while she took a boat out there."

She looked up from the scattered papers and photos. "So how do we play back what the stone recorded?"

"That's going to be difficult," I said. "The stone records onto the crystal, like a hard drive, but to read the recording requires a witch or a psychic who can pick up impressions from the crystal."

Felicity sighed. "She should have used a camera."

"Hey, it's magic, not science. I don't really want to go to the Blackwell sisters with the crystal. We don't know what's on it and I'm not ready to share it with anyone else." I thought for a moment. "There is a way we can see the recording but it means getting hold of a particular artifact. They might have one at the Society headquarters in Bangor."

"So let's get our hands on it," Felicity said. She seemed more gung-ho than usual and I wasn't sure if that was because she was so eager to work the case or because she was in a "go get 'em" mood.

"Make a call to the Bangor HQ tomorrow," I said. "Tell someone there that I need them to send over a Crystal Reader. In the meantime, let's go through all this stuff and see if we can piece together what Sherry was up to before the church massacre."

Felicity held up a photo of a slender black woman in a leather jacket approaching a door that bore the words *WESTLAKE P.I.* in black lettering on frosted glass. I recognized the door. It was the one that now said *HARBINGER P.I.* and led to my office. "I assume this is Sherry," Felicity said. "She's in most of the photos and they look like they've been taken from a distance, probably with a zoom lens."

I sat next to her on the floor and examined the other photos. Nearly all of them showed the same woman. In some, she was standing next to a blue Jeep. In others, she was simply walking along Main Street and I assumed Wesley had taken those pictures through his store window. There was one photo of Sherry standing at the edge of

Dearmont Lake, looking out over the water toward Whitefish Island.

Felicity was poring over the handwritten and typed papers. "These are records of when and where Wesley saw Sherry."

"Try to find any mention of the church or Clara," I said. "And don't forget the pizza."

We each took a slice and began to eat while we went over Wesley's notes. From what I read, it seemed like he'd decided to follow Sherry around every now and then to see if she would unknowingly lead him to material he could print in the *Observer.*

He wasn't successful. Most of the time he followed Sherry, she managed to lose him. I wondered if she had known he was tailing her and had taken evasive action or if Wesley had just been bad at following her.

He did follow her to the lake a couple of times and on December 21st, he saw her hire a boat from the marina and sail out onto the lake. He did the same and followed her from a distance, watching through binoculars as she placed the Apollo Stone in the bushes on Whitefish Island. After she'd returned to the marina, he had gone to the island and found the stone but, not knowing what it was, had left it there after taking photos of it. Those photos were on the floor along with the ones of Sherry and a couple of snaps of the lake that included the island.

Wesley had also discovered that Sherry was visiting Clara but not through any detective skill of his own;

someone in the grocery store had casually mentioned seeing Sherry's Jeep heading to Clara and Wesley had overheard the conversation.

There was no mention of the church in his notes and no photographs of it, so I assumed he'd never made a connection between it and Sherry. Nor had he seemed to realize that Sherry was tailing Mary Cantrell for a while. But then Wesley's own tailing skills were so bad that he probably hadn't considered that the subject of his investigation was tailing someone herself.

The notes seemed to end on December 22nd, which must have been when Sherry warned Wesley off by threatening him.

By the time Felicity and I had read all of the material and studied the photos, the pizza was gone and we'd drunk a couple of beers each.

"Another beer?" I asked her as I put down the final piece of paper.

"Yes, please." She was leaning back against the sofa surrounded by photos and papers.

I went to grab the beers from the fridge and realized how gloomy it was in the house. I opened the kitchen blinds to look outside. It was growing dark.

When I got back to the living room, Felicity had replaced everything except the Apollo Stone inside the cardboard box. She was still sitting on the floor, leaning back against the sofa, so I handed her a beer and joined her.

"Well that wasn't very illuminating," she said.

"All I learned is that Wesley would make a terrible detective," I said.

She laughed softly. "Yes, I got the same impression."

"Maybe the Apollo Stone will tell us more."

"I'll call the Bangor headquarters tomorrow and get them to send us a Crystal Reader," she said, as if reminding herself.

I took a swig of beer and leaned back heavily against the sofa. I was beat. "How many hours have we spent going over this stuff?"

"Too many," she said.

"Welcome to the exciting world of preternatural investigation." I raised my bottle and Felicity clinked hers against it.

We both drank. "You hungry?" I asked her.

"After that pizza? God, no. You aren't still hungry, are you?"

"No, not really. I just wanted to make sure I was being a good host."

"You are a good host, Alec. You're perfect."

"You think this is good, you should see how I treat my dates."

"I'd like to," she said, and then added quickly. "I mean, I imagine you treat them very well." She looked away, embarrassed.

Well, this wasn't awkward. How had the conversation gotten onto the subject of dating? *Remember, she's just broken up with her boyfriend*, I reminded myself.

"How did you get involved with the Society?" I asked her, bringing the conversation into safer territory. "Usually it's a family connection but your parents didn't do any work for the Society, did they?"

"No, not that I know of. They're Egyptologists but their work is strictly academic, not practical. I think they'd die of shock if they knew that the magic of ancient Egypt was being used today. They'd be shocked if they knew it worked at all.

"I didn't really find the Society, they found me. I was approached by a team of people who knew I was studying occult languages and wanted some help deciphering an Enochian text. It was a test. They were recruiting for the Society. They introduced me to some more people and I had to take more tests before I was told about the Society and given a job."

"And your first job was to come work for me."

She nodded. "And spy on you, as you found out within the first five seconds of meeting me."

"That wasn't your fault," I said. "I'm usually good at reading people."

She looked at me and arched an eyebrow. It made her look cute and…and I had to stop thinking like that.

"Can you read everyone you meet?" she asked.

"Hell, no. Most of my ex-girlfriends are still a mystery to me." There I went again, blundering into topics that might be best avoided.

But Felicity seemed intrigued. "Tell me about them."

"Who?"

"Your ex-girlfriends."

I shrugged. "What's to tell? As I said, they were a mystery to me. Of course, most of them thought that being a P.I. was just a way to get money out of gullible people. They didn't believe in the supernatural world."

"You didn't try to convince them otherwise?"

"No, I'd never take away anyone's ignorance of the supernatural."

"You make it sound like ignorance is bliss."

"Maybe it is."

"Have you ever dated someone who did believe? Another investigator or someone who worked for the Society?" She leaned in a little closer and I could smell the enticing lotus flower perfume again. I found myself wondering where she'd applied it before coming over. Her neck, of course, and maybe lower. My eyes followed the graceful line of her neck and traveled down to where the plunging neckline of her black blouse revealed a lot of cleavage.

"I don't think that would be a good idea," I said, leaning my face closer to hers even as I said it.

"Perhaps not," she whispered. I could feel her breath on my lips.

There was barely a fraction of an inch of space between our mouths and I took the plunge and crossed that gap, kissing Felicity softly. She returned the kiss, closing her eyes and murmuring a satisfied, "Mmm," sound.

For a moment, I forgot everything—missing investigators, church massacres, and lake monsters. Kissing Felicity was the only thing that mattered.

Then she broke away and looked into my eyes, her own wide with surprise. "Oh, my God, that shouldn't have happened."

She was right, it shouldn't. We were both emotionally raw right now: Felicity because of her recent breakup with Jason, and me because of Mallory's sudden departure.

We shouldn't have done it but that kiss had been amazing. It had felt so right even though it was wrong.

"I have to go," she said, getting up off the floor.

"You don't have to." I clambered to my feet. "I mean, okay, we agree that we shouldn't have kissed so let's forget about it and not let it affect our friendship."

She cringed when I said the word "kissed" and began toward the door. "I shouldn't have come over tonight, Alec. I wanted…well, I don't know what I wanted exactly but I should have stayed at home. I'm sorry."

"It isn't your fault," I said. "I'm the one who kissed you."

She opened the front door. Outside, the night was cool and dry. "We'll forget all about it," she said. "It never happened. Oh, God, I'm terrible at these things. I'm sorry,

Alec." She went outside and crossed the lawn, heading for her own at a record pace, not exactly running but not quite walking either.

"Felicity," I called after her.

"See you tomorrow," she said before fumbling her house keys out of her pocket and disappearing inside.

I closed the front door and then kicked it with my heel in frustration. What the hell had I been thinking? I'd even been telling Felicity how I thought that relationships between colleagues weren't a good idea when I'd moved in for the kiss. And now, I'd ruined a valuable friendship. I was a fucking idiot.

I went back to the living room and sank onto the sofa, lying down on it and facing the ceiling. Maybe I should call Felicity and apologize, but that might make things worse. She had said she was terrible at these sorts of things, and so was I. Calling her now wasn't a good idea. Maybe tomorrow, everything would go back to normal.

Who was I kidding? Things weren't going to just go back to how they were before. I'd fucked up again. What was wrong with me? First, I'd had a physical relationship with Mallory that had masqueraded as therapy and now I'd kissed Felicity. What a jerk.

My phone buzzed on the coffee table. I grabbed it and checked the screen. It was Mallory.

"Hey, Mallory," I said, trying to keep my tone light. She had enough problems of her own to deal with and mine paled in comparison.

"Hi, Alec. I got your message." She sounded the same as she had when she'd left, upset and depressed. I couldn't even hold on to the hope that in time she'd feel better. Time was something Mallory didn't have anymore.

"I was wondering how you are," I said. "And I wanted to say that if you ever need to come back here, the door is always open for you. You know that."

"Yes, I do. Thanks. I appreciate it."

There was an awkward pause, something that rarely occurred between Mallory and me. Then she said, "Alec, something's happened."

I sat up, wondering how Mallory could get herself into even more trouble than she was already in. It seemed to follow her through life ever since the Bloody Summer Night Massacre. "What is it?" I asked.

There was an even longer pause and then she said quietly, "Mister Scary."

"What? Have you found him?"

"I found his trail. Is your TV on?"

"No, I was working..." I found the remote trapped between the sofa cushions and pointed it at the TV.

"The news channel," Mallory said when the TV blared to life, showing a rerun of *Psych*. I found the news channel and stared in shock at the screen.

A blond reporter was talking to the camera while, behind her, ambulances and police vehicles sat in front of a large old house, their lights painting the scene blue and red and illuminating the grounds around the house, which seemed to be enclosed by a large wrought iron fence.

Police officers swarmed over the area, flashlight beams cutting the darkness. Yellow crime scene tape fluttered on the iron fence behind the reporter.

On the bottom of the screen, a caption read *Massacre in Abandoned House*. Scrolling beneath that were the words: *Killer attacks high school party. At least twenty dead. One female survivor.*

The reporter was saying, "...much like the Bloody Summer Massacre five years ago, although police won't confirm this. It is believed that the survivor managed to fend off the attacker and possibly kill him but when police arrived at the scene, he was gone." She paused and put a finger to her earpiece as she was fed information. "I'm now being told that the survivor is believed to be Leah Carlyle, a fellow student of the people killed here tonight."

A picture that looked like it had been taken from a high school yearbook appeared on the screen. It showed a dark-haired young woman smiling at the camera. The reporter's voice said, "Leah Carlyle is already being dubbed a Final Girl by the media, just like Mallory Bronson, the only survivor of the Bloody Summer Night Massacre five years ago. Whether tonight's atrocity was carried out by the same person, a man who referred to himself only as Mister Scary, remains to be seen."

I hit the mute button and said to Mallory, "What the hell?"

"He's done it again," she said. "He's created another final girl."

CHAPTER 9

I WOKE UP THE FOLLOWING morning with a hangover. The brightness of the morning sun beating through the window made me squint and hold my hand up to shield my eyes. It was half past nine. Felicity would be at the office already but she hadn't called me to wake me.

I sat up in bed and the movement sent spikes of pain through my skull. How the hell had I ended up with a hangover when I hadn't had all that much to drink?

Walking groggily into the bathroom, I got Tylenol from the cabinet and washed down two pills with water from the sink tap. I caught a reflection of myself in the mirrored cabinet door. I looked like shit.

I took a hot shower while I waited for the Tylenol to kick in and then dressed slowly, trying not to move my throbbing head too much, in a black T-shirt and blue

98

jeans. It wasn't until I got downstairs that I remembered I was working with Sheriff Cantrell today. Great. That was all I needed.

When I got downstairs and threw out the pizza box and beer bottles, I realized that I'd had more to drink than I'd thought.

Mallory and I had watched the news for a while and tried to guess what it might mean that Mister Scary had duplicated the Bloody Summer Night Massacre and created a second final girl. We couldn't come up with any answers that made sense but when Mallory hung up, she sounded a little brighter.

I think talking about it had been good for her and now she had picked up Mister Scary's trail again. Maybe this new killing would give her a clue that would lead her to him. I'd told her to call or visit anytime and we'd ended the call with our friendship on a firmer footing than it had been when she'd left here the other night.

After the conversation with Mallory, I'd had a couple more beers and watched the news a while longer, then had a couple more beers and thought about the kiss I'd shared with Felicity, then finally watched old episodes of *Castle* and had a couple more beers until I was too tired to keep my eyes open and I staggered up to bed.

My hangover didn't seem so implausible any longer.

I went up to the spare bedroom where I kept magical items and picked out the ones I might need today. A couple of faerie stones, an enchanted dagger, and a couple of potions that might help me find out exactly what happened to Deirdre Summers after she discarded her clothes on the shore of Dearmont Lake.

I stuffed everything into a black backpack and went downstairs, grabbing a pair of shades from the table by the front door before going out into the bright morning light. The Caprice roared to life when I turned the key and I winced when my head pounded in response.

I got to the station at quarter past ten and climbed gingerly out of the Caprice. Before I had a chance to cross the parking lot and go inside, I heard the sheriff's voice. "Harbinger, you're late."

I looked over to where he stood, leaning against his cruiser with a disgusted look on his face as he watched me approach. He was wearing shades too but I guessed it wasn't because his head was about to explode like mine was.

"What the hell happened to you?" he asked, looking me up and down.

"Nothing," I said. "Nice day, huh?"

He smiled humorlessly. "You've been drinking, Harbinger. Good thing I'm driving. Now get in." He opened the door and somehow got his considerable bulk through the gap and into the car. It wasn't that he was obese, although he certainly wasn't slim, but he had a huge frame that was packed out with muscle and fat like a bear. His uniforms were definitely custom-made and the size on the labels probably said "Grizzly".

I got into the passenger seat and put the backpack by my feet. There was a slight odor of sweat and corn chips in the car. Cantrell started the engine and the radio began playing country music. I cracked my window a little and he said, "Don't do that, we have air." He dialed it up and a cold blast blew into my face from the vent. At least I couldn't smell the corn chips anymore; now I could just smell dust.

As Cantrell pulled out of the parking lot and joined the traffic heading south out of town, I glanced out of the window at the Caprice, wishing I'd agreed to meet the sheriff at the lake and taken my own car. June and Earl's honeymoon car was way more preferable than being driven around in a police cruiser by a grizzly bear. That put a mental image in my head and I smiled.

"What are you grinning about?" Cantrell asked gruffly.

I looked over at him. "Are you the thought police now?"

"Don't push it, Harbinger."

I turned my attention to the road ahead and the throbbing in my brain.

"You have a party last night?" he asked.

"No, I didn't."

"You sure look like you did."

"I'm fine." I wanted him to stop talking. His voice and the country music coming out of the radio were making my headache worse.

He was quiet for a couple of seconds but then he ruined it by nodding to the backpack at my feet and asking, "What's in the bag?"

"Some things that may help us find out what happened to Deirdre Summers."

"Magical stuff?" Despite the fact that he'd seen magically-animated skeletons walking down Main Street, he sounded incredulous.

"Yeah, that's what I usually use in my line of work. Preternatural investigators and magical items sort of go together."

"Oh, I know all about preternatural investigators," he said ominously.

I kept quiet. I didn't want this conversation to turn into a "preternatural investigators killed my wife" rant.

But Cantrell was persistent. "You know Sherry Westlake?"

"I've heard the name," I said, glad that the shades were hiding my eyes. I had no doubt that a seasoned sheriff like Cantrell could spot a lie a mile away.

"I'm sure you know her," he said. "She's in the same line of work as you. Even had the same office. You all work for the same parent company, don't you?"

"I don't know what you mean."

"Well, I mean that there are preternatural investigators in most towns and cities. Now, I'm sure all those people didn't just get it in their heads one day to put up a shingle and go vampire hunting. It's a franchise, right? Like Pizza Hut or McDonalds."

He was right but the Society of Shadows was a secret society and I wasn't about to blow its cover. "If we were a franchise, don't you think we'd have matching uniforms or something?"

He chuckled. "Okay, if that's the way you want to play it, Harbinger, that's fine by me. I was just making pleasantries and talking to you about the woman who worked in Dearmont before you, that's all. Thought you might be interested. Unless you know already, of course."

"I don't know Sherry Westlake," I said truthfully. "I worked in Chicago before I came here. I didn't know anyone in the area when I arrived."

He nodded and pursed his lips, thinking quietly for a minute. "So how did you go from Chicago to here? Sounds like you got your ass kicked over something or other."

"Long story," I said.

We drove past Earl's Autos and Cantrell turned off the highway, guiding the cruiser along the road that led to the lake. He was quiet now, for a change. When we got to the parking lot where Felicity and I had sat in the Caprice and gone over the Deirdre Summers case file, Cantrell killed the engine and looked over at me.

"You definitely know about Sherry Westlake, and I don't just mean you've heard her name in conversation somewhere," he said.

I frowned at him, glad once again for the protection of the shades. "Why do you say that?"

"Because you never asked me what happened to her." He opened his door and got out.

I followed, cursing my hangover for taking away my common sense. Of course, when Cantrell told me that Westlake worked in my office before me, the natural thing for me to do would be to ask him why she left, what happened to her. The only reason not to ask him would be if I already knew about the church massacre and that Sherry was a suspect.

Cantrell stood looking out over the water, just as he had done in the photo taken three years ago, just after Deirdre Summers' disappearance. I wondered how much it rankled him that he hadn't been able to solve the mystery of the missing woman, particularly as she'd been a local and Cantrell probably saw her family in town every now and then.

He'd told me that he wanted to put the case to rest for the sake of Deirdre's daughter Natalie but maybe he also wanted to alleviate some of the guilt he felt at not being able to give the Summers family some closure.

I knew as well as anyone that sometimes cases remained unsolved. Leads vanished, witnesses died, or demons appeared and ate everyone involved. That was just the way it went and even though I didn't like John Cantrell, I didn't think he should blame himself for not solving Deirdre's disappearance, especially if there was a supernatural element involved. He couldn't be expected to account for that.

I, on the other hand, could. "Sheriff, did you bring the original drawings?" I asked him.

He turned to face me and nodded. "They're in the trunk."

I popped the trunk and found the drawings that Deirdre had pinned to her wall three years ago in a clear plastic folder. I put them into the backpack with the other stuff. "Okay, show me where her clothes were found," I said.

He locked the car and pointed to a trail that led from the parking lot into the trees by the lake. "It's this way."

I followed him, slinging the backpack over my shoulder. When we were on the overgrown trail beneath the trees, Cantrell said, "We have no idea why Deirdre came here that night. Her car was found in the parking lot, locked up as if she expected to return to it. That's one of the reasons that the suicide theory doesn't sit right with me. If she knew she wasn't coming back to her car, why lock it?"

"Maybe just out of habit," I offered.

He shrugged his big shoulders. "What do you make of those drawings?"

"It could be that she saw something at the lake one day and became obsessed with it," I said. "People who see things they can't explain sometimes develop an obsession with them. Did she ever mention seeing a monster?"

"Not as far as I know," he said. "When we interviewed Natalie, she said her mother had been acting a little strange but she couldn't explain the drawings on the wall."

We walked a little farther and then Cantrell stopped. "Here, this is the place." He pointed to the water's edge. "Her clothes were on those rocks there."

I stepped off the trail and went down to the edge of the lake. The water was calm, lapping against the rocks rhythmically. There was a smell of fish and weeds in the air.

I opened the backpack. Cantrell stood watching me from the trail. "What are you going to do?" he asked.

"Find out what really happened here," I said, removing the potion vials from the pack and putting them on the ground. "If you want to see too, you're going to need to drink one of these. You'll also have to look through the hole in this stone." I held up one of the faerie stones.

"What the hell kind of mumbo jumbo is this, Harbinger? I'm not drinking anything and I sure as hell am not looking through some damn stone. You trying to make a fool of me?"

I sighed and went up to him. "I thought you brought me on this case because of my special skills. You said you thought there might be a preternatural cause of death."

He nodded. "Yes, I did, but..."

"If we want to find a preternatural cause, we have to use preternatural means to do so," I told him. "Why did you invite me along? Did you think I was just going to get out a magnifying glass and look for clues?"

"No, of course not. But this is weird."

"I haven't even begun yet," I said.

He sighed and put his hands on his hips, saying nothing.

"Do you want to solve this case?" I asked him.

"You know I do."

I shook my head. "I'm not so sure. I thought it was strange that you hired me to work with you, especially after the zombie incident, which you blame me for. I think the Deirdre Summers case might just be a ruse to get closer to me and find out what I know about the subject you're really interested in: Sherry Westlake."

"No, that isn't right. I want to solve this case for Deirdre's daughter. Don't you dare question my motives, Harbinger."

"So shall I begin?" I said.

He nodded, determined to prove to me that he really wanted to solve this case. "Yes, do whatever it is you do."

"Are you going to drink the potion or not?"

He looked unsure about that. "I don't know. What's in it and why do I need to drink it?"

"Just herbs, water, and alcohol."

"Alcohol?" He eyed the vial suspiciously.

I rolled my eyes. "There's just a little bourbon in it. It's an old recipe that's going to let us talk to the trees."

He removed his shades and narrowed his eyes at me. "This is crazy."

"No, it really isn't. I'm going to use Deirdre's drawings to question the trees, kind of like when the police show photos to people on the street and ask, "Have you seen this man?" This is the same thing, except we're going to ask the trees if they've seen this monster." I held up the drawing of the lake monster.

"He's going to question the trees," Cantrell murmured to himself in disbelief.

"And the plants," I said, looking around at the undergrowth. "The ones that were here three years ago, anyway."

"This is crazy, Harbinger. You're crazy. I'm not playing along with this charade of yours."

I sighed. "Fine. I'll do it and I'll tell you what I see when I come back."

He frowned. "Come back from where?"

"Well, believe it or not, trees and plants don't speak English. The potion induces a vision state that lets me see what they show me. It'll be images and sounds, impressions left from when Deirdre was here. As well as the potion, I need a faerie stone to see the images. My magical tattoos aren't able to handle this."

Cantrell stood with his hands on his hips, his face looking up to the sky as if he were asking a higher power how he had managed to get involved in this craziness.

After a few seconds, he looked at me with a resigned look in his eyes. "Okay, what do we need to do?"

"Come and sit over here with me by the water's edge." I put Deirdre's drawings on the ground, placing small rocks on them so they wouldn't blow away in the summer breeze.

Cantrell sat down next to me and I handed him a faerie stone. He looked through the hole at the surrounding trees, as if expecting to see something that hadn't been there before."

"It won't work yet," I told him. "I need to say a few words and then we need to drink the potions. When I've done that, it takes a little time for the visions to begin. Use your left eye to look through the stone."

He switched eyes and glanced around.

"We need to be patient," I told him. "Trees aren't exactly in a hurry to go anywhere so they'll take their time."

He shook his head dismissively. "Harbinger, you should be in a psych evaluation ward, not living among sane people."

Cantrell was putting on a good show about not believing, but I could sense a lack of confidence in his voice. He was beginning to doubt his probably long-held belief that there was no reality beyond what you could see and touch in day-to-day life.

That belief had been eroded slightly by the appearance of the walking dead. What he saw once he took the potion and used the faerie stone was probably going to blow his mind.

I usually tried to protect skeptics from learning about the preternatural world, but in the case of Sheriff Cantrell, I would make an exception. In his job, knowing that there were more dangers in the world than just humans might save his life someday.

It would certainly make him a better sheriff because he'd look at every case that came across his desk from more angles, some of them outside the realm of mundane thinking.

I looked up at the trees and recited a short incantation that my friend Jim Walker had taught me when I'd been working with him in Canada. The words were so old that their origin was unknown but the incantation had been known in the Americas before any white man had ever set foot on the shore.

"Drink the potion," I told Cantrell as I popped the cap off my vial and downed the contents. It tasted bitter at first and then warm as the bourbon hit my throat. Cantrell drank his and put the empty vial on the ground.

He lifted the faerie stone to his eye and peered at the trees like a child who had just received a set of binoculars as a gift and was eager to try them out.

"Not yet," I whispered.

He sighed loudly. "You said we had to look through the stones."

"We do, but it isn't time yet."

"So how do we know when it's time?" His voice had dropped to a whisper to match mine.

"We'll know. For now, we wait."

The potion was beginning to take effect. My head, which had been pounding, now felt light and warm. The herbs suspended in the bourbon included hallucinogens and they were starting to kick in.

"I feel funny," Cantrell whispered.

I held up a hand to quiet him. A rustling sound was coming from the trees, as if they were being blown by a strong wind even though the day was only mildly breezy. The undergrowth also became agitated, leaves trembling like a rattlesnake's rattle as if they were trying to warn us of something.

I took off my shades, picked up my faerie stone, and glanced through the hole. Everything looked almost the same as it did before except it was nighttime. A full moon hung over the lake and the stars were bright in the cloudless night sky.

"Whoa," Cantrell said, and I assumed he had picked up his stone and was looking through it.

The night scene was quiet except for the sound of someone approaching, their feet swishing through the long grass at the side of the trail. I turned the stone toward the trail and saw Deirdre Summers there. She stood on the dark trail for a moment, watching the lake, before stepping out into the moonlight and walking to the rocks close to where Cantrell and I were sitting.

"This is incredible," Cantrell whispered.

"Be quiet," I told him.

"Why, she can't hear us, can she?"

"Of course not, this is just a recording. But I want to hear what's happening without you whispering into my ear. There might be something important."

"Right, a clue," he said knowingly. I wondered how much effect the potion had had on him. He sounded like he was stoned.

I looked over to check on him and because I had the stone to my left eye and had opened my right, I got a weird double vision effect. My left eye was looking at a night scene where Cantrell was not present so I was looking at grass and rocks; my right eye was looking at Cantrell sitting on the grass and rocks in bright sunshine.

I lowered the stone for a moment. "You okay?" I asked him.

"Yeah, I'm fine," he said, waving me away with one huge hand.

I raised the faerie stone to my eye again and went back to watching the night that Deirdre Summers had disappeared. She was standing ankle-deep in the water now, her gaze fixed on Whitefish Island in the distance.

The wooded island was dark, as if the silver moonlight couldn't reach it, despite the water around the island reflecting the full moon and glittering in its light.

Something moved on the dark island, a shadow within a shadow, and I heard a splash out there as whatever it was entered the water. It sounded big.

"What was that?" Cantrell whispered urgently.

"I don't know," I answered. I swallowed hard, fear rising inside me even though I knew that I wasn't present in this scene and was actually sitting by the lake in broad daylight on a summer's day three years later.

Deirdre was totally calm. She walked to the rocks and began to take off her clothes, folding each item and placing it neatly on the rocks. When she was naked, she returned to the water and waded in up to her waist.

There were still splashing sounds in the distance and they were getting closer. I was breathing hard, willing Deirdre to get out of the water. Didn't she realize she was in danger? What was she thinking?

Cantrell must have been having the same thoughts as me because he whispered, "No, get out of there."

Deirdre couldn't hear him, of course. She moved farther into the lake until she was in so deep that she had to swim. With an unhurried breaststroke, she swam out toward the distant sounds, her arms cutting through the moonlit water gracefully. She was so calm that I wondered if she'd been hypnotized or glamored.

"What is she doing?" Cantrell whispered. "What is she doing?" I could hear the stress in his voice.

Then, out on the lake, there was a movement that made the water roil and splash. A huge dark shape rose

113

from the water where Deirdre was swimming and engulfed her in blackness. I saw a frog-like eye and the dark bulk of its body for a fleeting second but then it was gone, sinking back into the depths.

Deirdre was gone too. The only thing that remained of her was the neat pile of clothes on the rocks. The huge creature's movement had caused a disturbance in the lake that sent waves splashing against those rocks and over the grass where Cantrell and I sat. I couldn't feel the water, of course, but I had an urge to stand up to avoid getting wet.

Cantrell had dropped his faerie stone and was getting to his feet unsteadily, his eyes full of terror. "What the fuck was that, Harbinger? It ate her. What was it?"

"Sit down," I said. From my faerie stone, I could hear movement in the night scene. Someone was approaching. "Something else is happening," I told Cantrell. "Pick up your stone."

"I don't want to see anything else like that...thing."

"I hear a person," I said. "There are footsteps on the trail."

He looked toward the trail.

"Not now," I told him. "Then. Use the stone."

He stayed standing but he picked up the stone and put it to his left eye.

The sound of footsteps that were accompanying the vision stopped momentarily and then continued, this time coming toward us over the grass. I turned my head toward the sound and saw a young dark-haired man wearing a black hoodie with the hood pulled up over his head. His eyes shone unnaturally bright blue through the shadows that fell over his face. He walked to the water's edge and stared out over the lake.

"You recognize him?" I asked Cantrell.

"No, I've never seen him before."

The young man held up his arms in a V shape and threw his head back to look up at the night sky. He began to chant in a language I'd never heard, a language that contained glottal sounds and weird combinations of consonants. I wished Felicity were here; she'd probably recognize the language and be able to translate it.

When he was done chanting, the hooded man turned from the lake and walked back to the trail before heading to the parking lot.

"Can we follow him?" Cantrell asked. "Maybe we can get a license plate number or something."

I shook my head. "Only the trees around here are working under the spell. If we move out of this area, we'll lose the vision completely." I lowered the faerie stone and opened my right eye, blinking against the sudden brightness.

Cantrell was sitting on the grass again now, his stone lying on the ground by his hand. He was gazing out over the lake toward Whitefish Island. "No wonder we couldn't find a body," he said. "That monster ate her."

"She was a sacrifice," I told him. "Whoever that guy in the hoodie was, he offered Deirdre to the monster, maybe as a part of some bargain."

"But why did she just swim out there to meet her fate? I don't get it."

"She was under a spell," I said. "She probably had no idea what was happening."

Cantrell frowned and murmured, "What am I going to tell Natalie?"

"Maybe this is one occasion where the case should remain unsolved." I collected the stones, empty potion vials, and drawings, and put them into the backpack. "Officially, of course. We'll solve it ourselves but it will have to be off the book."

"That's how you work, isn't it, Harbinger? Off the book. Hell, you don't even have a book."

I ignored him and slung the backpack over my shoulder. "We're done here. Deirdre was killed as a sacrifice to that monster. We need to find the guy with the bright blue eyes and deal with him."

"Wait a minute. What about the monster? It lives on Whitefish Island. We need to call the National Guard or the Army or someone like that to blow it up."

"No, we don't. The monster isn't on the island. It doesn't live in this realm of existence. It was summoned here to collect its sacrifice. Now it's gone back to wherever it came from until it's summoned again."

"So that's it? We just walk away after watching that monster kill Deirdre?"

"I'll take a look at the island," I said. "There might be some evidence there that can lead me to the guy in the hoodie, but it's outside your remit, Sheriff. There's nothing you can do to catch this guy by conventional means."

"Don't patronize me, Harbinger. If you're going to that island, then I'm coming with you."

That was all I needed. But Cantrell was like a dog with a bone and he wasn't going to let this go. "Okay," I said. "Get the department to hire a boat sometime and we'll sail out there and take a look around."

"We're going now," he said, putting his shades back on and marching back to the trail.

I followed him, resigned to the fact that I was going to be spending most of the day with Cantrell whether I liked it or not. I checked my phone to see if Felicity had called. She hadn't. I hoped she didn't think I was avoiding her by being away from the office for so long. Maybe I should call, check that she was okay. I put the phone back into my pocket. Later, maybe.

Cantrell was on a mission, striding quickly across the parking lot despite his size, heading for the docks and the boat hire places there. I followed him to a shack that had a sign in the shape of a wave proclaiming it to be Woody's Boat Hire.

Sitting outside the shack on a fold-up chair was an old man wearing a faded Portland Pirates cap and dark blue coveralls. He had a bushy white beard and was smoking a pipe. When he saw Cantrell, he nodded. "What can I do for you, Sheriff?"

"I need a boat that'll get me out to that island, Woody," Cantrell said.

The old man looked out at Whitefish Island. "Well, any boat will do that. You want a speedboat? Or something a little slower, maybe? You planning on doing some fishing?"

"I don't care what boat it is just so long as it has an engine," Cantrell told Woody.

Woody nodded sagely. "Not in the mood for rowing, eh?"

Cantrell jerked a thumb at me. "He'd be the one doing the rowing and I don't think he'd get us all the way there and back by sundown."

The old man looked me over. "I wouldn't be so sure. He's a big feller." He knocked ash out of his pipe against the arm of his chair and stood up slowly, rubbing his back and wincing. "Anyway, I have just the thing, a twenty-eight-footer with twin outboards. She'll get you to that island in no time."

He went into the shack and came back with a set of keys and a clipboard. "Just sign here, Sheriff."

"I don't have time for that," Cantrell said, snatching the keys from Woody's hand. "Just charge it to the department."

"But someone has to sign the hire agreement," Woody said, bewildered, watching as Cantrell went striding along the dock in search of the boat.

"Here," I said to Woody, "I'll sign for it."

He shrugged. "Okay, mister." He handed me the clipboard. I quickly wrote my details in the relevant boxes and signed at the bottom.

When I passed the clipboard back to him, Woody tore off my copy of the hire agreement and gave it to me. "It sure is a shame about the sheriff," he said. "He's been that way since his wife died last year. He's a good man beneath that gruff exterior. Losing Mary hit him hard. Damn shame, if you ask me."

"Yeah," I said. "Don't worry about the boat, I'll bring it back in one piece."

"Harbinger, what the hell are you gassing about?" Cantrell shouted from the end of the dock. "And which of these damn boats is ours?"

If he'd bothered to look at the paperwork, he would know that the boat we were taking out was called the *Princess of the Lake*.

I found her and held out my hand to Cantrell. "Give me the keys, I'm driving."

"The hell you are."

I held up the hire agreement. "I'm the only one of us insured to take her out onto the lake." I was pretty sure he was still under the effect of the potion he'd drunk earlier and I didn't want him to crash the boat into the island.

"You told me back there that you do things by the book," I said. "I hired the boat so I'm driving. And you're still under the influence of that potion. You wouldn't go driving under the influence, would you?"

He hesitated before throwing the keys at me. I caught them and began untying the *Princess of the Lake* from the dock. She was a simple fishing boat with a pale turquoise hull and a control console at the bow beneath a fiberglass roof.

Cantrell climbed aboard, muttering, "It's not called driving, you idiot, it's piloting. You pilot a boat, you don't drive it." He found a seat in the stern and sat down with arms folded over his barrel chest.

I *piloted* the boat away from the dock and out onto the lake. There were a few other craft on the water but the area around Whitefish Island was clear. The island stood alone—dark, brooding and waiting.

I looked back at Cantrell. He had removed his sunglasses and turned his face to the sun, eyes closed. Either he was trying to catch some rays or he was sleeping off the potion. I was pretty sure it was the latter from the way his chest rose and fell slowly. He'd probably be snoring soon. Well, he shouldn't bother getting too comfortable because we'd be at the island in five minutes, tops.

I checked my phone again. Nothing. No call from Felicity. After a moment's hesitation, I called her, deciding to play it cool and nonchalant. "Hey, Felicity," I said when she answered. "I'm just calling to see how everything is going. See how you are."

"I'm fine, Alec. Are you with the sheriff?" Her tone was a little flat but sometimes that was the norm for her so I couldn't tell if she was giving me the cold shoulder or just being her usual British self.

I looked back at the sleeping form of Cantrell. "Yeah, I'm with the sheriff."

"Have you found out anything regarding Deirdre Summers?"

"Yeah, a bit. We're heading for that island in the middle of the lake."

"All right, be careful."

She obviously didn't want to talk right now, so I said, "Okay, I'll see you later."

I was about to end the call when she said, "Alec, something's happened at the office."

"What? Are you all right?"

"Yes, I'm fine. It's just that when I got here this morning, the door was unlocked. You locked up last night, didn't you?"

I tried to remember. I'd been carrying the box of stuff from Wesley but I was sure I put it down on the sidewalk and locked the door. "Yeah, I locked up. Has someone broken in?"

"We haven't been burgled," Felicity said. "I mean, the computers are still here and nobody tried to break into the safe or anything."

"So what's wrong?" Maybe I had forgotten to lock up after all.

"There's one thing missing," she said. "A book. It's gone from the shelf in your office. There was a space where it should have been."

"Someone broke in and took a book?" It was true that some of the books on my shelf were rare and valuable but why would a thief only take one? Why not take all of them and the computers too while they were at it?

"Yes," Felicity said. "It's the only thing that's missing, I'm sure of it. I checked the titles on the shelf against the inventory I made when I put the books in your office. There's only one title missing. "

"So what book is it?"

"It's a book of black magic written in the Middle Ages. The *Grimoire of Dark Magic*. I was going to call you earlier but…I didn't."

"No problem. When I'm done here, I'll come straight back to the office. Do we need to call a locksmith to fix the door?"

"No, the door is fine. I used my key to make sure."

"Someone probably picked it."

"But what about the wards?"

The office was magically warded against things like break-ins. A mundane thief wouldn't have been able to cross the threshold even after picking the lock. "We're dealing with someone who was able to slip past them," I said.

"That isn't good, Alec."

"No, it isn't. And what makes it worse is that they now have a powerful book of black magic."

CHAPTER 10

AFTER ENDING THE CALL WITH Felicity, I pulled back the throttle on the *Princess of the Lake*. We were close to the island and I didn't want to crash the boat onto any rocks that might be lurking beneath the water or get her stuck in shallow water.

Cantrell was snoring now. The potion had hit him hard but I was sure he'd be fine when he woke up. Because I was more experienced with taking potions, the only effect I'd experienced was that my hangover had disappeared entirely. Maybe I should market the stuff as a hangover cure and make a fortune. The only problem was, the FDA definitely wouldn't approve of some of the ingredients.

I cut the engine and let the boat drift, looking for a good place to go ashore. Whitefish Island was mostly wooded, with rocks and fallen trees littering the shore.

There was no obvious place to land a boat, and certainly not a 28-footer.

I looked over the side of the boat and frowned. I could see the bottom through the clear water and there were rocks down there. I was still thirty feet from the shore but it looked like I was going to have to swim the rest of the way. Great.

I dropped the anchor and waited while it dragged on the bottom of the lake for a couple of seconds before settling. Then I took off my jeans and T-shirt, socks, and boots. When I was down to my boxers, I climbed over the edge of the boat and lowered myself into the water. It was damn cold.

Letting go of the boat, I swam for the island. I'd made the right choice not bringing the boat too close to shore; the water was shallow in places and my feet bumped against rocks.

Tendrils of weed brushed against my legs and thoughts of the monster that had swum in these waters three years ago entered my brain, making me panic. "Just stay calm," I told myself. "That thing has gone back to wherever it came from."

When I reached the shore, I pulled myself up out of the water and sat on the rocks for a moment, glancing back at the *Princess of the Lake* and the sleeping sheriff in the stern. I'd be back on board before he even knew I was gone.

I wondered how Sherry Westlake had managed to get to the island and place the Apollo Stone here. Wesley hadn't mentioned that she'd taken a dip when he was watching her through his binoculars. Maybe she'd had a smaller boat and was able to anchor it right by the shore.

I checked my line of sight. If Wesley had been watching Sherry from the docks, that meant she must have been on this side of the island when she hid the Apollo Stone in the bushes. I walked along the shoreline, pine needles and dirt sticking to my wet feet, until I found a small rickety-looking dock. Damn, I could have made this so much easier on myself if I'd seen it earlier. I could have docked there and simply stepped off the boat, keeping my clothes on in the process.

Too late for that now. I was here, so I might as well take a look around.

The island wasn't very large, maybe a quarter mile across and a half mile long, so I could cover it in a short amount of time. Of course, I had no idea what I was looking for or even if I'd find anything at all. Evidence that a magical ritual had taken place here was the most obvious thing to look for but as far as I knew, the last time the monster had been summoned was three years ago, when it had eaten Deirdre Summers.

Since then, any number of people could have visited the island: fishermen, vacationers, teenagers looking for a quiet place to make out. And the weather could have destroyed any evidence that the blue-eyed man in the hoodie had been here. Three winters had passed since then.

I looked around anyway. There were no birds in the trees and the only sound as I searched the island was the crunching of pine needles and twigs beneath my bare feet. I found a bare patch of dirt and a circle of stones where someone had built a campfire some time ago but it wasn't the type of circle I was looking for.

After about an hour of searching, I sat on a mossy tree stump in the middle of the island, ready to admit defeat. If there had ever been anything of interest here, it was long gone by now.

So why had Sherry Westlake placed an Apollo Stone on the island? What was she hoping to record? As far as I knew, she hadn't been investigating the Deirdre Summers case. And even if she had been investigating that case, why would she put an Apollo Stone on the island now, three years after Deirdre went missing?

It didn't make sense. The only thing I was sure Sherry had been investigating was the church in Clara. So was the island connected to the church in some way? I thought about that for a while but couldn't come up with any answers.

Finally, I decided to give up on the island for now. I needed to return to the office. I also needed to eat. My stomach was growling hungrily. I got up and made my way back to the shore. When I reached the small dock and was just about to follow the shoreline around to where the *Princess of the Lake* was anchored, I stopped.

I turned and inspected the trees on the island. There were a few that had fallen over, uprooted by the wind, killed by disease, or maybe even hit by lightning, but they had all been felled by natural causes.

Except one. The stump in the center of the island, the one I had just been sitting on, had a flat top. It had been cut by a chainsaw.

I retraced my steps to the stump. It was in a small clearing with no sign of the felled tree anywhere. I searched around and found it eventually, a tall pine that had been dragged fifty feet away and left lying in the undergrowth. The cut at its base matched the stump in the clearing. Clean and straight.

Why had someone cut down this one tree and dragged it over here? I returned to the stump. Moss covered its top, which made it a comfortable place to sit. But what was hiding beneath? I found a stick and began scraping at the spongy moss, clearing it away from the top of the stump.

After a minute of scraping, I revealed a section of the wood beneath. Something had been carved into it. I could see a line and a curve that were definitely manmade. I went back to clearing the moss and when it had all been removed, lying in dark green clumps around the tree roots, I looked down at the stump.

Magical symbols covered every inch of the wood, carved at least an inch deep with a knife or some kind of woodworking tool. I examined them closely. They looked similar to the symbols in the stained glass window at the church. I couldn't check because my phone was on the boat. That meant I couldn't take photos of the carvings, either. I was going to have to swim back to the boat, take her to the rickety dock and come back here to get pictures.

I got back to the shore and waded into water, shivering at its cold touch. When I was up to my waist, I leaned forward and entered the water with a gasp before breaststroking my way back to the *Princess*.

Cantrell was still asleep and snoring heavily, his upturned face burning slightly in the sun. I started the engine and guided the boat to the small dock before slipping my feet into my boots, grabbing my phone from my jeans pocket, and treading carefully onto the wooden structure. It held under my weight but I wouldn't put any bets on Cantrell being able to stand in the wooden slats without them giving way beneath him.

I tied the boat to the dock and walked back to the clearing at the center of the island, hoping my boxers would dry off so I could put on my jeans when I got back to the boat. If Cantrell woke up and saw me coming out from the trees in my boots and boxers, he'd probably arrest me on some sort of indecency charge.

When I got to the stump, I turned on my phone and compared the symbols carved into the wood with the ones on the stained glass window at the church. Some of them were identical.

Whoever made this makeshift altar was using the same magical system that was being used by the robed figures in the church window. I couldn't deny a connection between the island and the church now. Sherry Westlake had somehow known about this tree stump altar last year and had put the Apollo Stone on the island to keep an eye on it.

I called Felicity. When she answered, I asked her, "Did you manage to track down a crystal reader?"

"Yes, they're sending one over from Bangor. It should be here today."

"Great. I found an altar here on the island and it's carved with the same symbols as we saw in the church windows."

"Oh, that's terrible," Felicity said.

"Terrible? No, it's good. We have a connection between Deirdre Summers and the church. We should be able to find more clues about what's been going on, why those thirteen people were massacred."

"Yes, I know that, but this language scares me, Alec. It only ever turns up where black magic or evil are involved. And it's been found throughout history all over the world. Whatever is going on here is bigger than we thought if someone is using that language as part of a magical system."

"We should know more when we get that reader and use it to play back the information on the Apollo Stone." That was assuming the Apollo Stone captured anything before Wesley Jones removed it from the island. But it had been here, recording, on Christmas Day so there might be something on the crystal that showed activity on the island while the massacre at the church was taking place.

"I'll be there soon," I told Felicity. "I need to get back to the boat and put on my clothes before Cantrell wakes up."

"What?" She sounded shocked. "What exactly is going on there, Alec?"

"I'll tell you all about it later."

"Okay," she said. "Be careful."

"I will." At least being so deep into the case gave us things to talk about that didn't involve last night's kiss.

I ended the call and took some photos of the tree stump altar before heading back to the dock. Cantrell was awake and standing in the boat with his hands on his hips, watching me as I approached.

"What the hell are you doing, Harbinger?"

"I decided to go for a swim," I said.

"In your drawers?"

"I didn't bring my trunks." I climbed onto the boat and began to get dressed. Cantrell was staring at me. "What?" I asked, pulling on my jeans.

"That's a hell of a lot of ink you've got there. I was looking at it, that's all," he said defensively.

"Magical protection tattoos," I said. "My version of a bulletproof vest."

He nodded, continuing to watch me as I dressed. "That job of yours come with a gym membership too?"

I pulled my T-shirt over my head and said, "I train at home. I have to stay in shape, my life may depend on it."

Cantrell might have had a comeback if this conversation had taken place this morning before he saw the monster in the lake. Now, he knew the kind of enemies I dealt with. He simply nodded and kept quiet.

"Anyway," I said, "while you were sitting here catching flies, I was searching the island. I found an altar. It was probably used to summon that creature we saw."

"Did you destroy it?"

"No, it's abandoned, overgrown with moss. Whoever made it hasn't been here it in some time." I started the boat's engine and untied the mooring line. When we were clear of the shallow water and rocks, I opened up the engine and left the island behind.

Cantrell was strangely quiet, his eyes gazing into the distance, a thoughtful look on his face, all the way back to the dock. Even when I gave the boat keys back to Woody and thanked him, Cantrell offered only a cursory nod to the old man before following me back to the cruiser in the parking lot.

"You okay?" I asked him when we reached the vehicle.

He snapped out of it. "Of course I am. I'll drop you back at the station so you can pick up your car." He got in and started the engine. Country music came drifting out of the radio. Cantrell turned it off when we hit the highway and said, "Thanks for your help today but I can take it from here."

"We're nowhere near solving the case yet," I said. "We don't even know who they guy in the hoodie is."

"I'll find that out using good old-fashioned police work. We know what happened to Deirdre now, which is what I asked you to find out. You did that, so thanks."

"I can help catch that guy," I said. "Don't kick me off the case before it even gets started."

"I'm not going to argue about it, Harbinger. As far as you're concerned, this case is closed, do you understand?" He shot me an angry look before turning his attention back to the road.

I didn't say anything but cracked my window open.

"I told you not to do that," Cantrell said, "We have…"

"Air, yeah, I know," I said, enjoying the fresh air blowing on my face through the open window.

CHAPTER 11

WHEN I GOT TO THE office, I had a paper sack of food under my arm. Cantrell had driven back to the station in silence, lost in his own thoughts, and after he'd dropped me by the Caprice, I drove out to Darla's Diner and got Sandra the waitress to bag up a couple of burgers and some fries. I was sure Felicity wouldn't have eaten yet today and eating lunch together seemed like a good idea. At least it might dispel any awkwardness between us.

She looked up from her computer when I leaned in through her office door and held up the sack of food. "That smells delicious, Alec. I haven't eaten at all today."

"I didn't think you had. Let's eat in my office. I'll open the windows so any clients we get won't drool from the smell and leave a puddle on the floor."

"Ewww, not a nice mental image when I'm about to eat." She got up and followed me into my office. She had gone back to wearing her usual office attire; a white blouse and black skirt. Her hair was piled up on top of her head in the usual manner too. The look said, "business as usual" but a mental image of her in the black lacy top and jeans flashed into my head.

I opened the windows in my office to let the warm breeze inside and tipped the food out onto my desk. "A cheeseburger and fries for you," I said, handing her the paper-wrapped packages, "and a Darla's Double Burger and fries for me." I slid a can of cold soda across the desk to Felicity and popped one open for myself.

There was an empty space on the bookshelf where the *Grimoire of Dark Magic* had once been. "Is anything else missing?" I asked Felicity as I took my first bite of the burger. The meat practically melted in my mouth.

"No, just that book. But if you look at all the other books, you'll see that they've all been pulled out of the shelf a little bit. I didn't move anything so you could see it exactly as I found it."

"The thief was probably searching them for the one he wanted. Probably using a flashlight. So he may have had to pull them out to examine the titles."

"But why would he put them back and only take the *Grimoire of Dark Magic*? If it was a normal burglary, there are books on that shelf that are worth stealing more than the *Grimoire*. Your edition of the *Grimoire* is a late edition

135

with all of the original Latin text translated into modern English. There's a first edition *Lesser Key of Solomon* there that's worth much more than the *Grimoire* on the underground market."

"Unless the thief didn't take the book to sell," I said.

"Yes, of course, I've considered that. The *Grimoire of Dark Magic* contains spells and formulas from the Middle Ages. It would be dangerous in the wrong hands, of course, but it would take a lot of magical knowledge to make those spells work. They're complex rituals and whoever wrote the *Grimoire* was vague regarding their use. The book is more an item of historical item interest than a practical spell book."

"Someone doesn't think so," I said, waving a handful of fries at the shelf. "They left all these other books behind and went for that one."

Felicity nodded and ate some of her cheeseburger. "How did you get on with Sheriff Cantrell?" she asked.

"I got kicked off the case."

"Oh? What did you do?"

"I didn't do anything." I told her about the trip to the lake, the vision of Deirdre Summers' death, the blue-eyed man in the hoodie, and the altar on the island. I finished off the story by saying, "And then Cantrell told me he was going to take it from here and that as far as I was concerned, the case was closed."

"That's odd, since he's the one who hired you in the first place. Are you sure you didn't do something to make him angry?"

"Yes, I'm sure. That man's default setting is angry. He was quiet all the way back from the island, though. I'm pretty sure he was thinking about his wife's death and wondering if it's related to the Summers case. If there's even a chance that there's a connection, he won't want me looking into the Summers case because it might lead to the church massacre."

"But we are looking into his wife's death."

"Yeah, but he doesn't know that. In fact, I think hiring me to work with him was just a part of his investigation into the church case. He was fishing for information about Sherry Westlake, like I know where she's hiding."

"If she's alive," Felicity reminded me.

I finished my burger and fries and gulped the soda down. "The police evidence seems to suggest she is. Besides, she's an investigator and we don't kill easily."

"You're all so tough," Felicity joked.

"Tough and charming."

She looked down at her burger for a moment then back up at me. "Speaking of charming, Alec, I think we should talk about last night."

"Okay," I said, "You want to go first?" The truth was, I didn't know what to say about the kiss we'd shared. It had been so damned good but the situation between us wasn't exactly uncomplicated.

"It's complicated," Felicity said, her words mirroring my thoughts. "I know I'm still getting over Jason and my emotions are all over the place but last night, I got it into my head that I knew exactly what I wanted and that was you. I came over to your place wanting that kiss to happen, Alec. And maybe more. But when it did happen, I panicked."

"There's no need to explain," I told her.

She threw her hands up. "I feel like there is. I don't regret what happened. But I don't want to ruin our working relationship or our friendship. With all that's been happening lately, my emotions are confused."

"Confusion isn't a good basis for starting a relationship," I said. I sounded like one of those calendars that has a pearl of wisdom for each day of the year.

"No, it isn't." Felicity let out a sigh. Then she looked worried. "I'm not saying I only kissed you because I was confused. I didn't mean that at all. What I meant was…"

I held up my hands to stop her. "Felicity, you don't need to explain anything. And it wasn't your fault. I kissed you just as much as you kissed me. There's something between us that goes beyond work and friendship and I reacted to it just as much as you did. But we don't need to rush in to anything. We can take our time, let things settle down a bit. We see each other every day and neither of us is going anywhere." I frowned and added, "You're not going anywhere, are you?"

Felicity grinned. "No, not this time."

"Okay, so let's just take it one day at a time." There I went again dispensing Harbinger's thought for the day.

She nodded. "That's fine with me."

"Great," I said. Hell, I was no expert on these things. My relationships were usually short and sweet because I lived in a different world from every girl I'd ever dated. Eventually, that put every relationship at breaking point and we went our separate ways.

But Felicity lived in the same world I did, a world where monsters, demons, and other creatures stalked the night. A world where magic was real and a battle between good and evil was fought every day. Life felt more precious because danger lurked around every corner.

Maybe it was possible to build something more than I'd known in the past.

A knock on the open office door made us both look up. A bearded man in a cream shirt and black pants stood there with a small cardboard box in his hand. "Alec Harbinger?" he asked.

"That's me," I said, getting up.

He put the box under his arm and produced a tablet from his belt, tapping away at it with a small plastic pen. He looked at the screen and then back at me. The image on his screen would be the photo that had been taken of me when I'd become an investigator.

Satisfied that I was indeed Alec Harbinger, he gave me the package and tapped at the tablet again before asking me to sign for the delivery. After he'd gone back down the stairs, I watched him through the open window as he got into a small, blue, unmarked van that was parked across the street and drove away.

"That was quick," Felicity said. "Was he a Society courier?"

I nodded. "The Society doesn't normally use the regular delivery companies. Its own couriers are much faster." I opened the cardboard box and placed it contents on the desk. The crystal reader was unremarkable in appearance, just a silver box with a depression on the top in which to place a crystal and a hole on one side to project the contents onto a wall or screen. There were no dials, buttons or switches. The device was enchanted and worked by using some sort of spell that was anchored inside the box.

"Would you like to come over to my place later for a special showing of Whitefish Island: The Movie?" I asked Felicity.

She smiled and nodded. "I'll bring the popcorn."

I almost said, "It's a date," but stopped myself. Instead, I said, "I was thinking of driving over to Clara this afternoon. Want to come?"

"You're going back to that creepy place again? What for?"

"I think I'll try to talk to the Fairweather family, the people who own the church. Maybe they know something about what happened on Christmas Day, something they haven't told the police. They don't sound like the type of people who would talk to outsiders."

Felicity looked incredulous. "So why would they talk to you?"

I shrugged. "They probably won't but I want to meet them face to face. Maybe I can pick up some vibes from them that'll give me a clue about what was actually being worshipped at that church."

"You think the church was dedicated to some evil deity?" she asked.

"You saw those windows."

"I don't buy it, Alec. Why would Amy Cantrell's mother get involved in something like that? And why did everyone in the church that day end up dead, including the pastor, one of the Fairweather family?"

"Black magic is dangerous."

Felicity didn't look convinced. "I'll come with you to Clara but I don't think the church was dedicated to evil. Mary Cantrell wouldn't have had anything to do with it."

"We never knew Mary Cantrell," I reminded her, picking up the Caprice keys.

"Do I need to change?" Felicity asked.

"Yeah, it might be a good idea. We don't know how nasty the Fairweather family might be to outsiders. There might be running involved."

She went into her office to change her clothes and I closed the windows before picking up the crystal reader and sliding it back into the cardboard box it had been delivered in.

The wards on the building would activate automatically as soon as the office was empty and locked up, but someone had already gotten past them and I didn't want to have to explain to a Society officer in Bangor why the crystal reader had gone missing while it was in my possession.

Felicity met me in the hallway, wearing a T-shirt, jeans, and sneakers. The T-shirt was blue, tight-fitting, and had Outpost #31 across the chest in white stenciled letters.

"You a fan of John Carpenter's *The Thing*?" I said as I led the way down the stairs.

"Who isn't?" she asked.

"Well, at least I've confirmed that you have good taste in movies." I locked the office door and we walked around to where the cars were waiting.

"You've confirmed it, have you?" she joked. "It didn't exactly take any investigative skill on your part. All you had to do was look at my chest."

"Err, yeah." I unlocked the Caprice quickly. "We'll take my car."

"Wait a minute," she said. "Are you armed?"

"I've got an enchanted knife in a backpack." I reached into the back seat and held it up to show her.

Felicity nodded slowly and got into the car. She didn't say anything but I knew what she was thinking. I should be carrying the knife. I took the sheathed weapon out of the backpack and attached it to my belt. I hadn't been kidding about the Fairweather family earlier; they could be trouble, especially if they ran some sort of monster-worshipping cult.

When we got onto the highway headed east of Dearmont, I got that feeling again that I was being watched. Checking the vehicles in the rearview mirror, I made a mental note of the colors and models. If we were being tailed, it would soon become obvious, especially once we took the road to Clara.

After almost an hour of driving along the highway and constantly checking the traffic behind us, I took the turn toward Clara. As we drove along the tree-lined road, I checked the rearview again and saw nothing but empty road behind us.

Maybe I was just being paranoid. For the rest of the journey, as I navigated the Caprice around the narrow roads that wound through the trees, we were alone.

The six ramshackle houses came into view and I pulled over and killed the engine.

"What are we going to do?" Felicity asked, peering at the houses through the windshield. "Just go and knock on one of the doors?" Her voice had lowered to barely more than a whisper.

"Seems like a good place to start," I said. My own voice was at whisper-level too. There was an atmosphere among these quiet houses that made me think that if I spoke too loudly, I might wake up something that was sleeping in the gloomy woods. Something that would be better left asleep.

I took the crystal shard out of my pocket and slid it out of its pouch onto the dashboard. It glowed bright blue. "That creepy feeling," I told Felicity, "I think it's a spell. Good way to keep strangers out. Anyone who comes down here is going to just keep driving until they're far away from this place and the creepy vibe it gives off."

I got out of the Caprice and closed the door softly, reassuring myself that the dagger was within easy reach by letting my fingers brush over the leather sheath.

Felicity joined me and we walked over to the nearest house. The place was set back from the road a little behind an overgrown lawn that was more weed than grass. A gray stone path was losing a battle against an army of crabgrass. We walked along the path and up three rickety wooden steps onto a porch that leaned to one side at such a steep angle, I felt like I might slide off it and into the weeds.

I knocked on the front door and stepped back, taking Felicity's arm and leading her to the edge of the porch.

"What are you doing, Alec?"

"These people might have a 'shoot first' policy. I'd rather we weren't in the line of fire."

But after a couple of minutes, it was obvious that nobody was even going to answer the door, much less shoot us through it.

"Maybe no one is in," Felicity said.

I wasn't so sure. "Let's take a look around the back." I stepped down off the porch and followed the side of the house to a rear area that was just as overgrown as the front. A dilapidated barn sat at the far edge of the property and there was a large pond beside it, green algae floating on the water. A smell of mold and stagnant water hung heavily in the air. Beyond the barn and the pond, the woods were dark.

"You hear that?" I whispered to Felicity.

She nodded. "Frogs."

From the pond, there came a series of croaking sounds that I was sure had only started since we'd come around the back of the house.

"Let's check out the barn," I said, moving toward it through the weeds that seemed to grab at my legs.

The rear door of the house burst open and an old woman with long gray hair stepped out onto the rear porch, leveling a shotgun at us. She wore a yellow dress and I was sure she was the same woman who had stared at me as I'd driven past the house after searching the church.

She didn't say anything. The shotgun told us everything we needed to know.

Two bearded men came out onto the porch, armed with revolvers. They wore loose shirts and jeans and they were both big and burly with similar facial features, definitely brothers. One of them spoke. "You need to leave now before you get hurt."

"I just want to ask you some questions," I said, keeping my voice level and calm.

"We don't answer questions," the other brother said.

The old woman spat. "He's that supernatural investigator from Dearmont, the one Luke warned us about."

"I don't know anyone named Luke," I said. "I just want to find out what happened to one of your family, Simon Fairweather, and the other people in the church. Maybe you can help me do that by answering a few questions."

She grinned toothlessly at me. "Oh, we know what happened to them, mister. We don't need no fancy investigator coming here and telling us our own business."

"Okay," I said. "So maybe you know what happened to a colleague of mine, another investigator. She was at the church that day."

"We don't know what happened to Sherry Westlake. She was an interfering bitch and I hope she's dead. Or worse." The calm voice came from the direction of the barn and I turned to see the young man with the piercing blue eyes I had seen in the vision at the lake. He was wearing a black hoodie just as he had been at the lake.

He walked with a calm air of authority. Despite his age, the other family members probably bestowed him with his authority because he possessed greater power than they did.

"I assume you're Luke," I said. "So are you going to tell me what happened on Christmas Day?"

He halted ten feet away from me. "Yes, I am Luke Fairweather, But as for the glorious events of Christmas Day, I'm not sure you'd understand." He stroked his chin thoughtfully and looked into my eyes. "Or maybe you would. The police and the FBI had no idea what they were dealing with, of course. But you, Harbinger, you're different. You know what can come to this world when the veil is torn, don't you?"

"I've seen a few things," I said. I wasn't sure how he knew my name but I guessed that any self-respecting black magic practitioner like him would be aware of who the local preternatural investigator was.

He grinned at me with an amused expression on his face. "Yes, I'm sure you have. I can see it in your eyes. You've seen the dark things in this world."

"Seen them and killed them," I said.

The amused look vanished from Luke's face. "You're a blasphemer, Harbinger. Killing the creations of the Dark Mother is a sin." The frog chorus grew louder, filling the stagnant air with angry croaking sounds.

I shrugged. "If killing frog-eyed monsters is wrong, then I don't want to be right."

Luke Fairweather shook his head in disgust. "You're a filthy blasphemer just like my father. He led the church but he never truly believed. Well, he learned the error of his ways when he was sacrificed to Gibl. Now he is one of the thirteen, writhing in eternal agony for the glory of the dark gods."

Dark shapes began to emerge from the pond and clamber up onto the weeds and grass. Frogs of all colors and sizes. There must have been thousands of them, hopping and crawling toward us, their croaks growing louder as they got nearer to us.

Luke smiled. "I suggest you leave."

Felicity and I both stood our ground. "I haven't finished here yet," I said.

He sighed as if bored with me. "Yes, you have." Nodding to the people on the porch behind us, he pointed at me and then turned back to the barn.

I heard a shot crack through the air and felt a hot stinging sensation in my left side. The impact knocked me off my feet and I tumbled into the long grass, clutching at my side. When I inspected my hand, it was covered in blood.

"Felicity, get out of here," I shouted.

But suddenly, she was standing over me, looking down at me with panic in her dark eyes. "Alec!"

I fumbled for the dagger at my belt and managed to draw it from the sheath. The glow from the blade bathed the long grass around me blue.

"Can you move?" Felicity asked me. "No, you shouldn't move. I'll call an ambulance."

"I'm not staying here," I said, struggling to my feet. Pain flared in my side and I gritted my teeth against it, forcing myself to ignore it. Felicity helped me over to the side of the house, where I leaned on the wall for support. The three Fairweathers had gone from the porch and there was no sign of Luke. He had obviously gone back to his barn. Frogs swarmed over the entire area, turning the ground into a carpet of jumping and crawling wet, slimy bodies.

I managed to get to the Caprice and hand Felicity the keys. "You're going to have to drive." I felt light-headed and I wondered how much blood I'd lost.

She helped me into the passenger seat and got behind the wheel, adjusting the seat to accommodate her shorter height while saying to herself, "Eastern Maine Medical Center. That's the closest."

She cranked the engine and spun the steering wheel, turning the Caprice around in a flurry of dust, smoke and squealing tires.

Felicity floored the accelerator and the Caprice shot away from Clara like a bat out of hell.

CHAPTER 12

ALMOST FOUR HOURS LATER, I was sitting on a hospital bed at the Eastern Maine Medical Center watching night fall through the window. I wasn't in the bed wearing a hospital gown or anything. After being poked and prodded by doctors, X-rayed, and put on a morphine drip, I was fully-clothed and sitting on the bed. The staff looking after me were all Society members, trained to deal with things like demon venom, magical attacks, and faerie enchantments.

Felicity had called the Society's Bangor headquarters while driving me over here and told them that an investigator would be arriving at the medical center. When we'd arrived, the Society team at the center had tended to me immediately. The doctor in charge of my care, a friendly, bearded man named Dr. Davis, had been disappointed that my wound was a simple mundane gunshot wound.

Now, after being bandaged up and sitting on the bed for hours, I was more than ready to go home. The pain in my side had eased and apparently the bullet had gone straight through flesh and muscle and come out the other side, avoiding anything vital in the process.

The door opened and Dr. Davis came into the room with a large manila envelope in his hand. There was a confused look on his face. "Alec," he said, standing at the foot of the bed, "the X-rays have come back from radiology and there's something I'd like to show you."

He flicked a switch to illuminate the light panel on the wall but before attaching an X-ray to it, he took a sheaf of papers from the envelope and passed them to me. They were pictures of X-rays of what looked like a child's ribs.

"Do you remember when you fell out of a tree at age four and your parents took you to the hospital because they thought you might have fractured your ribs?" Davis asked.

"I was told about it, but I don't remember it," I said. "I was too young."

He nodded and pointed at the papers in my hand. "Those are copies of the X-rays you had done back then. Your ribs were only bruised, as it turned out."

"Yeah, they look okay in these pictures," I said, wondering if there was a point to Davis showing me X-rays of my four-year-old ribs.

"They do, don't they? I got those from your medical records after I saw the X-rays from today. You see, at first I thought the radiographers were playing a practical joke on me when they sent me your X-rays today. Then, after I went to their department and talked to them, and they assured me there was no joke, I got them to check the machine to see if it was faulty. It wasn't."

"I'm not sure I understand what you're saying, Doc. Is there something wrong with my ribs?"

He looked perplexed. "I don't even know how to answer that question, Alec. It might be better if I show you. Maybe you can explain what I'm seeing." He fixed a series of X-rays to the light panel and stepped back so I could see them.

Felicity gasped. I just sat there and stared, shocked.

The X-rays showed my ribs as white against the dark background but there was something else, something that wasn't in the X-rays that had been taken when I was four years old.

The bones had magical circles and symbols etched into them. The circles and symbols showed as an even brighter white on the bone, almost as if they were glowing. They covered every bone visible on the X-ray.

Dr. Davis said, "I can see from your reaction that you know nothing about this."

"No, I don't. How is it possible?"

"I have absolutely no idea. Certainly not by any medical procedure. This has to be magic. The lines that form the symbols are no thicker than a hair's breadth and the depth of the cut is even less than that. This is magical artistry, performed by someone with great skill and accuracy."

I had a pretty good idea how the markings had gotten onto my bones. My father had already had the Coven erase some of my memories, so why not have them inscribe my bones with magical symbols too?

But I was sure this would have been done before the memory wipe. It was probably because of these symbols that I was able to summon the power to kill DuMont. They were the reason I had been able to hurl a ball of energy at Tommy the bully when I was nine years old. The memory wipe had been my father's attempt to make me forget that incident. So the markings on my bones must have already been there when he got the Coven to lock my memories away.

How many times had my father taken me to the Coven and had them cast an enchantment on me?

I remembered something Devon Blackwell had said to me, and grinned.

"What is it, Alec?" Felicity asked.

"When the Blackwell sisters told me I was enchanted, I said their runestone might be picking up on my tattoos. Devon said no, the enchantment was much deeper than that. I didn't realize she was being literal. It doesn't get much deeper than being in your bones."

Dr. Davis said, "Alec, you know I have to report this. Society protocol says I have to report any abnormality found in an investigator's condition, especially if that abnormality is caused by magic."

"Yeah, you can report it," I said, "but the Society already knows about this. Well, my father does, anyway, and he's a member of the Inner Circle. This isn't something that happened to me recently; those marks have been there since before I was nine years old."

"Still, this is the first time I've seen them and they aren't on your last set of X-rays so…"

"Yeah, go ahead and report it. In fact, make sure the report goes to Thomas Harbinger, my father." Might as well let Dear Old Dad know that I'd discovered his handiwork.

Davis nodded. "Yes, I can do that."

"So can I leave now?"

He pointed to my side. "How do you feel?"

"I feel great," I lied. Actually, the bullet wound wasn't painful as long as I didn't move much but every now and then it throbbed and sent pain lancing through my hip and back.

"I'll get a nurse to bring in the discharge forms for you to sign." He shook my hand. "Good to meet you, Alec."

As he was about to leave the room, I said, "Hey, Doc, make sure that report goes straight to Thomas Harbinger."

CHAPTER 13

WHEN FELICITY PARKED THE CAPRICE in my driveway, a light rain had begun to fall, spattering on the windshield and pinging off the car's roof. Felicity had insisted on driving me all the way home, despite me telling her that if she wanted to collect her Mini from town, I could drive myself the rest of the way from there.

"Do you want me to come in with you?" she asked after turning off the engine.

"No, I'll be fine," I said. "I'm going to go straight upstairs and crash on the bed. You should do the same. It's been a long day."

"I will. Are you going to be coming in to work tomorrow?"

"Hell, yeah. It takes more than a bullet to keep me down." I gave her an "Everything's fine" grin that I wasn't sure she could see in the darkness.

"All right," she said, opening her door and handing me the car keys. "You can drive us to the office, then. How does eight o'clock sound?"

"Early." I opened my door and got out, pleased that I only felt a little pain in my side. Maybe I'd feel worse once the morphine wore off. But for now, at least, I was good. The night was cool and the rain felt like ice-cold needles against my face. "You should get inside quickly," I told Felicity. "This rain is going to come pouring down pretty soon."

She closed her door and nodded. "See you in the morning, Alec."

I watched her walk along the small stretch of sidewalk to her house next door and waited until she'd gone inside before going to my own front door and opening it.

As soon as it was open, I knew something was wrong.

The hairs on the back of my neck and arms stood on end. Someone had slipped through the magical wards I'd placed on the house. I listened carefully. The house was silent except for the hum of the AC and the fridge.

Stepping back onto the driveway, I pulled my phone from my pocket and called Felicity. She answered immediately. "Alec, is everything all right?"

"Yeah," I said. "I'm just checking you're okay."

She laughed softly. "You just watched me go into my house."

"And everything's okay in there?"

There was a second's pause and then she said, "Are you trying to get me to invite you over?"

"No, nothing like that. I'm just checking on you."

"I'm fine. I'm sitting in front of the TV with a glass of orange juice, watching infomercials."

"That doesn't sound fine to me."

"I'll see you in the morning," she said. Then she added, "Thanks for checking on me, Alec. It's nice."

"No problem. I'll see you in the morning."

"Is everything okay?" she asked, her tone more serious.

"Yeah, I'm just heading inside now. Enjoy the infomercials." I ended the call and considered taking the enchanted dagger from my belt before entering the house but decided against it. If there was someone hiding in there, I didn't want to advertise my location by holding a glowing blue weapon. For now, it could remain in its sheath on my belt. If I needed it in a hurry, I could get to it easily enough.

I pushed the front door all the way open and stepped into the darkness of the house, closing the door quietly behind me. The intruder wasn't going to get out easily, I'd see to that. Standing motionless, I listened again to the house. Everything was quiet.

Then I heard a noise upstairs. It was barely audible and I had to go to the foot of the stairs to hear it again but when I heard it a second time, I recognized it. The sound of paper sliding against paper, like the pages of a book being turned.

As well as the tomes and grimoires I kept at the office, I owned a larger collection that was currently housed in the spare bedroom at the back of the house. So now I knew the intruder's location. And if they were still looking though a book up there, they had no idea I was home.

Ascending the stairs as quickly as I could while still remaining quiet, I felt my heart hammering in my chest. Adrenaline was flooding my body, working with the morphine to take away the pain in my side completely. I was on edge, ready to fight.

When I got to the top of the stairs and looked along the hallway, I could see a faint light coming from the spare bedroom. A flashlight beam within the room. That would be my first target. My plan was simple: take away the intruder's light so it couldn't be shone in my eyes and then attack in the darkness. And keep attacking until my opponent was subdued and ready to tell me that the hell he was doing in my house.

I could hear the pages of the book continuing to turn slowly. The intruder still had no idea I was here. I crept forward, arms raised, fists tight.

I reached the open door and took a split second to peer into the room and see a hooded figure bent over one of my tomes, the flashlight beam pointed at the page, before entering the room low, fists raised, and lashing out at the flashlight with my foot. It went spinning into the air, its beam flickering over the walls, floor and ceiling like a crazy strobe light.

I moved to the side quickly, avoiding a fist that came hurtling in my direction. I threw a punch at where I thought the intruder's face was but now the flashlight had landed in the corner of the room, its beam pointing at the wall, leaving the rest of the room in darkness. I had planned to use the darkness to my advantage but hadn't figured on the intruder fighting back so adeptly.

A punch connected with my shoulder and slapped the arm away before shooting forward, staying low. I grabbed the intruder's hips and twisted my body to bring him down to the floor. I was rewarded with a karate chop that connected painfully with my upper back as my opponent wriggled free.

He fled into the hall and I caught sight of a black hoodie like the one Luke Fairweather wore. I gave chase, diving for the intruder's legs before he could get downstairs and out of the house.

We tumbled together down the stairs, struggling against each other and throwing wild punches that didn't connect with anything. The stairs slammed into my back, legs, and shoulders and I hoped they were causing the same amount of pain to the intruder. Maybe the fall would slow him down and I'd be able to subdue him once we reached the floor.

When we reached the bottom step, my opponent was up on his feet at lightning speed and reaching for the front door. I hooked my arm around his boot, bringing him crashing to the ground. By the time he had scrambled back to his feet, I was facing him, crouching low in a fighting stance, my hands raised and ready to go into action. "There's no point running," I said.

Instead of running, he adopted a fighting stance that mirrored my own. He was shrouded in shadow, hood pulled up, face hidden. His stance told me he meant business, but so did I. One of us was about to receive an ass-kicking.

He moved first, chopping the side of his hand through the air toward my throat. I blocked it and sent a kick arcing at his torso. He managed to block it with both hands but couldn't grab my leg, which was what he'd tried to do. The force of the kick knocked him into the living room, where he regained his composure and repositioned himself into a fighting stance.

I moved forward quickly, planning to knock him down with a couple of blows to the head followed by a fist to the solar plexus. But when I made my move, each blow was blocked. He went on the counter-attack, fists flying through air at various parts of my body. I blocked a face strike and a kidney punch and a double-fisted chop that would have knocked me down had it connected with my throat.

When the intruder decided to attack using a high kick to my face, I seized the opportunity to duck low below the fast-traveling booted foot and then come up quickly beneath the extended leg, pushing it high into the air and sending my opponent crashing onto the coffee table. The table held and the black-hooded figure rolled backward off it and out of my reach.

I adopted the fighting stance again and waited.

Instead of attacking, the intruder held up a hand and said, "Okay, Harbinger, time out." Her voice was feminine and that took me by surprise.

I lowered my guard slightly. "Who are you?"

She pushed the hood back to reveal an attractive face beneath shoulder-length curly black hair. "I'm an investigator like you. My name's Sherry Westlake."

CHAPTER 14

I HELD UP MY HANDS and said, "I don't want to hurt you, Sherry." She was definitely the same attractive black woman I'd seen in the photos Wesley had sent over. I had assumed that because she was a fugitive, she'd have run far away from Dearmont but here she was.

"You don't want to hurt me?" she said. "You're a little busted up yourself, Harbinger. I'd say I was holding my own."

I couldn't argue with that. "Okay, we'll call it a draw," I said, trying to lighten the atmosphere. "But there's no need for us to be fighting at all. We're on the same side. At least, I think we are."

"I hope so," she said. "Because right now, I'm risking my life just being here. You know the FBI is after me, right?"

"Yeah, I know. You want to tell me about it?" I indicated the sofa.

"Bring me one of those beers from your fridge and I'll consider it." She sat in the easy chair and waited while I got two bottles of Bud.

I sat on the sofa, facing her across the coffee table I'd thrown her onto earlier. "Why didn't you just tell me who you were as soon as I found you upstairs?"

"I'm trying to lay low," she said. "I needed to come here to check out your books because I couldn't find what I needed in the grimoire I took from your office. That's been returned, by the way. It's upstairs with your other books."

"Okay, thanks, but what were you looking for in it?"

She held up a hand. "I'll get to that in a minute." After taking a swig of beer, she said, "I fought back because I didn't know if I could trust you. I still don't. I wanted to get in here, find what I wanted, and get out without getting caught. When you attacked me, I figured I could still get out of here without you recognizing me. But, it wasn't to be." She sighed and took another pull on the beer bottle. "You should have stayed in the hospital for longer."

"You knew I was in the hospital?"

"I've been following you ever since I saw your picture in the newspaper. It stood to reason that a P.I. doing my old job would end up looking into that church sooner or later. I need someone I can trust to help me and you seemed like a good candidate. Once I found what I needed from your books, I probably would have contacted you one way or another."

"If you need help you should contact the Society," I said. "What makes you think you can trust me?"

She shot me an incredulous look. "The Society? Have you heard what's happening to the Society lately? There's a witch hunt going on involving senior members, and talk of spies from some medieval group that want to throw the civilization back a thousand years. I couldn't go to the Society in case I ended up talking to one of those crazies."

"So why trust me? I could be working for the Midnight Cabal for all you know."

Sherry laughed. "Oh, that's a good one. If you were one of the spies inside the Society, you wouldn't have had your ass busted from Chicago all the way down to an office in Dearmont. You'd be trying to rise up the ranks and get deeper inside the Society's infrastructure, and that would mean not getting tossed to the smallest town in America that has a P.I. So unless you're the worst spy in the world, I'm pretty sure you aren't working for any Midnight Cabal. Is that what they're called?"

I nodded.

She finished her beer and set the empty bottle on the table. "Look, the only reason anyone gets sent here is because they're on the Society's shit list. I think the only reason they set up an office here is to use it to punish investigators gone bad. As far as the Society is concerned, this is a preternatural dead zone." She pointed at me. "But you and I know different."

"Yeah, we do. So when you say investigators gone bad, are you including yourself in that description?"

She smiled and nodded. "Yeah, I definitely fit that description. And so do you. Otherwise you wouldn't be here. You and I have more in common than just our good looks and kickass fighting style."

I laughed. "You know, despite the fact that you're a fugitive from the law, you're actually easy to get along with."

"You should see me when I'm not being chased by the FBI. I'm the life and soul of the party."

"You want another beer?" I asked her.

"Sure, but how about we eat some of that lasagna from your freezer too?"

"Did you check out all of my food supplies when you broke into my house?"

She put on a mock offended look. "Broke in? There's nothing broken, I picked the lock as lightly as a butterfly landing on a flower and it opened for me."

"You broke through the wards."

She shook her head. "My tattoos broke through your wards. I didn't do anything."

"I'll get the beers," I said. "And I'll put the lasagna in the oven. But I want information. I need to know exactly what happened at the church on Christmas Day."

ADAM J. WRIGHT

"Don't worry, I'll tell you. Like I said, I need some help, and now that we've been introduced, I'm sure my hunch was right and you're the right guy for the job."

I went into the kitchen and put the oven on while I got the lasagna out of the freezer. I grabbed two more beers from the fridge and shouted to Sherry, "Do you mind if I call Felicity, my assistant, and get her to come over? She's been helping me with the church case."

Sherry was standing right behind me, leaning against the wall with her arms folded across her chest. "Sure, why not? I mean, it's not like I'm trying to lay low or anything."

"I trust Felicity with my life," I said. "She won't tell anyone you're here."

She thought about it for a moment and then shrugged. "Go ahead and call her."

I handed her a beer and got my phone out of my pocket. Felicity answered immediately. "Alec, is everything all right?"

"Yeah, fine," I said. "Listen, something's come up. I think you should come over here."

"I'll be there right away," she said, and ended the call.

"She's coming over," I told Sherry.

"Great. I'm going to go get something from my car. It'll help explain what I'm going to tell you." She disappeared out of the front door and into the rainy night.

I slid the lasagna into the oven and leaned against the kitchen counter while I drank my beer. The gunshot wound was beginning to ache so I took a couple of

Tylenol and washed them down with some Bud. I had tender areas on my arms where I'd blocked Sherry's blows earlier and I was sure I'd have bruises tomorrow. Sherry was some fighter.

As an investigator, she had been trained to survive in adverse circumstances, which was why I didn't bother asking her how someone on the run from every law enforcement agency in the country had managed to procure a car and stay under the radar for seven months. She was a resourceful woman.

Felicity came through the open front door, shaking rain from a pink umbrella outside before closing it and placing it by the door. She was wearing the same jeans and sneakers she'd worn earlier but had changed out of the Outpost #31 T-shirt and put on a peach-colored blouse with a red string tie at the collar. Her hair was loose, covering her shoulders like a dark silky mane. She looked amazing. She smelled amazing too, her perfume a subtle scent of jasmine and orange blossom.

She definitely hadn't put that blouse on just to watch TV at home.

"That top looks great on you," I said as she came into the kitchen.

"Thanks," she said. "I got it in London. Are we having lasagna? It smells good." She smiled, her dark eyes lighting up, and I suddenly felt sorry that Sherry was here. I mentally kicked myself for being so vague on the phone. Felicity had the wrong idea about why I'd invited her over.

167

"Listen," I said, "the reason I called…"

"When it rains, it pours," Sherry said, coming in out of the rain and shaking droplets from her hair. She held a blue shoe box in one hand. When she saw Felicity, she waved. "Hi, Felicity."

Felicity looked over at her and then back at me. "Alec, what's going on?"

"Felicity, this is…"

"Sherry Westlake—yes, I know," she said. Then she whispered, "What is she doing here?"

"I caught her looking at my books in the bedroom."

"What?" Felicity looked confused.

Sherry came forward and put her arm around Felicity's shoulder, guiding her into the living room. "You come and sit down with me and I'll explain everything while Alec gets you a beer."

"Tea, please," Felicity told me over her shoulder as she was led away.

I made tea for Felicity and took it into the living room where Sherry had reclaimed the easy chair. I sat on the sofa and waited while she recounted everything she had told me—which wasn't really much—to Felicity.

When she was done, she picked up the blue shoe box and put it on her lap. She took out a newspaper clipping and laid it on the coffee table. The headline read THIRTEEN DEAD IN BIZARRE CHRISTMAS DAY SLAYING. Beneath the headline, there was a black and white photo of the church at Clara.

"Before any of this happened," Sherry said, "I was already investigating that church. In late November, the sheriff's wife, Mary Cantrell, came to the office and told me she wanted to hire me to investigate the place. I asked her why and she said there was something weird going on there. Black magic rituals and that kind of thing. Obviously, I told her I'd take the job."

"Mary Cantrell hired you?" I asked. "We were under the impression that you were following her."

Sherry frowned at me. "Who told you that?"

"Her daughter."

Understanding flickered in her eyes. "Ah, that makes sense. Let me tell my story from the beginning and you'll see why the Cantrell girl thought I was following her mother."

"Okay," I said, picking up my beer and relaxing back into the sofa.

"I went to the church," Sherry said, "and my eye of Horus tattoo lit up like it was the fourth of July. There was a serious glamor over that place. Have you seen those windows?"

"Yeah, we saw them," I said.

"Felicity too?"

Felicity nodded. "Yes, I saw them through a faerie stone."

"Then you know the kind of thing we're dealing with here. I dug through some old local records and found out that before there was even a church in that location, those

ADAM J. WRIGHT

woods had been used by some sort of black magic cult that
worshipped a beast they called Gibl. There are reports of
monster sightings in that area going back hundreds of
years. The place got a reputation for being cursed centuries
ago and nobody went into those woods during the
daytime, never mind at night."

She got some more papers out of the shoe box and laid
them out on the table. They were photocopies of
newspaper pages from the late nineteenth century and all
of them had stories about a creature sighted in the woods
around Clara.

"And this is the really interesting one," she said,
pointing to a page of the Dearmont *Observer* that had the
headline *LOCAL CHURCH STRUCK BY LIGHTNING*.
There was a grainy photo of the church, a black burn mark
traveling from its roof and along the wall to the ground. A
number of men stood by the church, smiling at the
camera.

"Look at this guy here," Sherry said, pointing to a lone
figure skulking by the church doors. Unlike the others, he
wasn't smiling; his face looked sullen. Despite the grainy
quality of the picture, I recognized the young man
immediately.

"Luke Fairweather," I said.

Sherry nodded. "Uh huh. Now look when this
photograph was taken."

I checked the date on the top of the page. June 21, 1932. I looked at Sherry. "So what is he? Vampire? Faerie?"

She shook her head. "From what I can tell, he's a human being who is being kept alive by black magic. I think something happened that day when the church got hit by lightning. After that, a lot of people left the congregation. Now, I know some folk around here are superstitious, and having a church struck by lightning might be seen as some sort of divine disapproval but I think there's more to it than that. I think this is the moment the place became evil. Look at the church window in that photograph. You can just see the edge of it there."

The photo showed the edge of one of the stained glass windows. The scene on the window was of the crucifixion of Christ.

"What do you see?" Felicity asked.

"We see the same as you," I told her. "The crucifixion."

"You see, I think the church was normal until the day it got hit by lightning," Sherry said. "It was built in a cursed wood where there had been monster sightings since forever and the family that ran it was odd but I don't think there was anything evil about the church until that day in 1932. And I discovered a record from 1934 that listed the pastor of the church as Pastor Luke Fairweather."

I pointed at the photo of the lightning-struck church. "That lightning was probably the result of some spell Luke had cast, maybe to show off his power to the other members of the Fairweather family. They gave him the job of pastor and he took the church down the road he wanted it to go in all along, the worship of the creature called Gibl."

"But why would they do that?" Felicity asked. "If they were normal God-fearing people, they wouldn't hand the church over to a monster-worshipping black magician."

"You aren't taking into account how black magic corrupts those whose lives it touches," Sherry said. "Once he got them involved in the dark arts, they would become addicted to its power like it was heroin. And Luke had some sort of immortality thing going on so as the older members of the family passed away, he could corrupt the next generation and the next until the entire family became worshippers of this Gibl creature. It was all they knew. And anyone who didn't fall into line probably became a monster snack."

"And that's what happened to Simon Fairweather on Christmas Day," I said. "Luke considered Simon an unbeliever so he made him part of a thirteen-course dinner for Gibl."

"Along with Mary Cantrell and eleven others," Felicity said. She looked at Sherry. "I don't understand what Mary was doing at the church. You said she hired you to investigate it but her daughter told us Mary was a member of the church—obsessed with it, in fact."

Sherry sighed and her brown eyes saddened. "When I told Mary about my research into the church, she insisted that she wanted to help me take it down. She offered to go undercover and find out what she could from the inside. I couldn't have done that myself because Luke would instantly know who I was.

"I told Mary no, but she said if I didn't help her, she'd go undercover and investigate the church by herself. I got the impression that she thought she had something to prove to her family. Her husband was the sheriff, her daughter a deputy, and I think Mary wanted to make them proud of her by taking down some bad guys herself.

"So I said I'd work with her on the case. I didn't want her to go wandering in there by herself and get hurt. Every time she was going to the church or meeting with other members of the congregation, she'd let me know and I'd follow her. I was trying to protect her more than anything else, making sure she didn't get into trouble."

She finished her beer and put the empty bottle on the table. "It didn't turn out that way. Mary infiltrated the group too well and when twelve people from the congregation were chosen to attend a special Christmas Day service, she was one of them. She called me on Christmas Eve and told me something big was going down and we might be able to kill Gibl. Up until then, all we'd

ADAM J. WRIGHT

uncovered was a bunch of crazy people praying to a monster.

"I wanted to kick down the church doors and start busting heads but there was nothing I could act on, no evidence that the pastor and the congregation weren't just deluded. Mary said the pastor had assured the twelve chosen ones that Gibl would make an appearance on Christmas Day so I figured if that monster was ever going to appear, that was the time."

She paused, sniffed the air, and said, "I think that lasagna's ready."

"I'll go get it," I said.

"I'll help you." Felicity followed me into the kitchen. When we got in there, she whispered, "Alec, if Cantrell finds out that Sherry is here, you'll be arrested for harboring a fugitive."

"So he won't find out," I said, grabbing the oven mitt and taking the lasagna out of the oven. I got three dishes and began slicing the pasta into three portions.

"You don't seem too bothered about it," Felicity said.

"Cantrell is in a world of his own right now, trying to figure out if there's a connection between the death of his wife and what he saw happen to Deirdre Summers. He's probably hoping the two aren't related because nobody wants to think of their loved one being eaten by a monster."

She sighed. "Well, just make sure you don't get in trouble over this. I don't want to have to visit you in prison."

"You'd visit me?" I asked.

"Of course. I'd bake you something every day."

"It might be worth going to prison just for that," I said with a smile.

She narrowed her eyes at me. "I bake for you all the time as it is. I always bring food to the office."

"Not every day, though. And if I went to prison, you'd have to add an extra ingredient."

"What's that?"

"A file."

Felicity rolled her eyes and went to hit me playfully on the shoulder. I caught her forearm and pushed her back gently against the wall, keeping her arm pinned above her head. Our faces were close, so close I could feel Felicity's breath against my mouth.

Her dark eyes looked into mine for a second and then she closed them and leaned forward slightly. We kissed. She tasted of sweet tea and lip gloss. I released her forearm and Felicity lowered her hand so her palm pressed against mine, our fingers entwining.

Sherry's voice came from the living room. "A girl could die of hunger around here."

We broke the kiss and looked into each other's eyes as we laughed. I reluctantly let go of Felicity's hand and stepped back, dazed by what had just happened. "Wow," I said.

Felicity grinned. "Yeah, wow."

"We should get that lasagna to Sherry," I said.

Felicity nodded. "Definitely."

I handed her a dish and followed her into the living room with the other two and some forks.

"What were you two doing in there?" Sherry asked. "Making kissy-face at each other?"

Felicity looked at me sheepishly and I was sure a similar expression was on my face.

"Oh, sorry," Sherry said, holding up her hands in front of her face and turning her head to one side. "None of my business."

We sat on the sofa and I handed Sherry her lasagna and a fork. She tasted the food and closed her eyes in satisfaction. "Mmm, that's good. Now, where were we?"

"You were telling us about Christmas Day," I said.

"Oh, yeah. So, I waited on Mary's street in my Jeep until she came out of her house and got into her husband's Dodge Ram. It had been snowing heavily so I guess she wanted to take the pickup in case she needed to use the four-wheel drive. I followed her over to the church but I stayed a mile or so behind her because I wanted everyone to be in the church by the time I got there. That way, I could park my Jeep with the other vehicles and get my stuff out of the back while they were all busy in there doing their thing.

"When I got to the church, everyone was inside. I got out of the Jeep and opened up the back. I had an enchanted sword and a crossbow with silver-tipped bolts. I had no idea what would kill the monster and my research didn't reveal anything specific so I planned to get some ranged attacks with the crossbow and then move in with the sword. The enchanted blades kill just about everything."

She took another bite of lasagna and waited until she'd swallowed it before continuing. "I shut the Jeep and stood there for a while for something to happen. There was chanting coming from inside the church and, even though I didn't recognize the language, I knew it was some kind of summoning spell. So I moved closer to the doors, ready to run in there if the summoning succeeded and Gibl appeared. That's when I heard screaming and the sounds of bodies being thrown against the walls. I pulled the doors open and rushed inside, sword in hand, ready to slice up anything that wasn't human.

"The place smelled of blood and sulfur and there were bodies lying on the floor, as well as pieces of broken furniture. In the center of the room, there was a dark bulky shape that stood as high as the church ceiling. I couldn't make out any features because it was fading slowly, returning to whatever hell it came from. Luke Fairweather was standing by the altar, magic sparking from his hands. I knew who he was because Mary and I had researched the entire family and Mary said that even though Simon was the current pastor of the church, she got the feeling it was Luke pulling all the strings."

"That makes sense," I said. "Luke thought Simon was a blasphemer and sacrificed him to Gibl."

"Well, here's something that doesn't make sense," Sherry said. "I started sprinting across the church with my sword ready and all the time I was telling myself that it was crazy to attack a magician like that. I expected a bolt of energy to come flying out of his fingers and blow me away at any second. But that never happened. Luke turned tail and ran through a door at the rear of the building. I heard voices outside and figured the rest of the family was coming to inspect the monster's handiwork. So I went back to the Jeep and got out of there.

"As I was heading back up that road that leads to the houses, I ran into some kind of magical barrier blocking my way. So I turned off the road and drove into the woods but there wasn't any trail I could follow and eventually I got stuck among the trees. I walked to the highway and hitched a ride from a passing trucker. Next thing I knew, my face was on the TV and the FBI was hunting me."

"The sheriff and his daughter arrived at the church and found the bodies," I told her. "All of the circumstantial evidence pointed to you. Amy knew you'd followed her mother to the church that day and when the police found your Jeep and it looked like you'd fled, they put two and two together."

"And came up with five," Sherry said.

"I don't think they take monsters from other realms into consideration when they carry out their investigation," I said. I ate the last forkful of my lasagna and then waved my fork at Sherry. "What were you looking for in my books?"

She put her plate on the coffee table and leaned toward us. "Luke Fairweather isn't done killing yet. That's why he ran when he faced me at the church instead of blasting me to pieces."

"He's saving up his magical energy for something big," I said. "He could have blasted Felicity and me when we were at his house but he chose to let one of the family shoot me instead."

"Whatever he's up to," Sherry said, "the church massacre was only a part of it. There's more to come. I was checking your books to see if I could find any black magic rituals that involve killing thirteen people."

"There are lots of them," Felicity said. "Thirteen is a powerful magical number."

"Yeah, I discovered how many there are when I looked through the *Grimoire of Dark Magic*." Sherry shook her head. "So we're back at square one. I was hoping to find which particular ritual or formula he's following so I could predict when he's next going to cast a spell and deplete some of that energy he's been storing up. At the moment, he's so full of power that attacking him would be suicide. When he releases some of that magic into a spell, that would be a good time to strike."

Felicity closed her eyes and her brow furrowed. She began reciting something to herself.

"You okay?" I asked her.

"I'm mentally going through all the rituals I know of that require a sacrifice of thirteen victims," she said. "Maybe I can find one that specifically requires a sacrifice of thirteen people in a church."

"Has she got a database in her head?" Sherry asked, pointing at Felicity.

"She has a good memory," I said.

Felicity opened her eyes and sighed in frustration. "It's no good, there are too many."

"How about the altar on the island?" I asked. "Do the symbols help to narrow it down?"

Felicity shook her head. "No, but if I knew which spell Luke used to summon Gibl, I might be able to work out the ritual he's following." Her eyes widened as an idea came to her. "Of course, why didn't I think of it before? We might be able to find out exactly which spell he used. It should be on the crystal from the Apollo Stone."

"You have my Apollo Stone?" Sherry asked.

"Yeah, it's in there." I pointed to the cardboard box in the corner of the room.

She went over to the box and took out the Apollo Stone. "Do you have a crystal reader?"

I nodded. "In the car."

"Okay, so let's fire it up and see what's on here." She took the crystal from the center of the stone and held it up to the light. "It's recorded something because the crystal has gone cloudy. When there's nothing on them, they're clearer."

"I'll get the reader," I said. I went out to the car and took the box out of the trunk. The rain had stopped, leaving the street glistening. The night breeze was warm and humid, tinged with the smell of night blooming jasmine in one of the nearby gardens. The smell reminded me of Felicity's perfume.

I took the crystal reader back inside and put it on the coffee table. "Are you sure this is going to show us anything useful?" I asked Felicity. "Luke summoned the monster at the church, not the island, on Christmas Day."

"No, he didn't," she said. "Not technically speaking. The reason he made that altar on the island out of a tree trunk is because he set it up as a permanent anchor point for Gibl to cross over into this realm. The tree is part of nature and it's better than a manmade altar for making a portal that's bound to a specific area. The summoning that took place at the church merely invited the monster to that location from the island."

"So Luke would have summoned it to the island first and it waited there until his second spell transported it to the church?" I asked.

Felicity nodded. "He would have needed to use a lot of power to summon Gibl from its realm to the church. Since he already had the portal on the island set up, it would be much easier to summon it there and then later use a minor summoning to get it to the church." She shrugged. "That's what I'd do anyway."

"It's worth taking a look," I said. Sherry handed me the crystal and I put it into the depression on the top of the reader, making sure the face with the projection hole was pointing at the wall. I turned out the lights.

A soft, blue glow emanated from the crystal and the box. A beam of blue light was projected on the wall. At first, nothing happened and we were all staring at a glowing blue square but then images formed like ghosts becoming corporeal. I saw trees, the sky, and the clearing on the island, all in blue monochrome.

Luke Fairweather appeared, trudging through the snow, his breath condensing in the air in front of his face. Instead of the usual black hoodie, he wore a padded winter jacket.

He cleared snow from the top of the tree trunk altar and mumbled a few words that were too low to hear.

"I can't hear anything," I said.

Felicity shushed me by putting her finger to her lips. The blue image on the wall was reflected in her glasses but I could still see her eyes, locked on the screen so intently that I wondered if she was trying to read Luke's lips.

"I know this," she whispered excitedly. "I'm sure I recognize it."

Luke stepped back from the altar and raised his arms, reciting words in the same weird language he had used at the lake three years ago.

Felicity seemed to understand some of it, at least. She was nodding at the words, taking them in.

Luke's voice rose as he seemed to be approaching to the climax of the spell. He flung his arms toward the sky again and shouted a sentence that included the word "Gibl" before stepping back to the edge of the clearing. Black smoke began to rise from the ground, twisting itself around the altar and the surrounding trees. It rose upward in a thick column, obscuring everything. Then the image flickered and ended. The blue glow dimmed slowly until it faded into nothing.

I got the lights and blinked against the sudden brightness when they came on.

I looked at Felicity, who was sitting very still, staring at the blank wall where the image had been. "Did you understand any of that?"

She nodded. Her voice was low and weak. "Some of it. Enough to know what ritual he's performing."

Sherry put a hand on Felicity's shoulder. "Are you okay, honey?"

"This is really bad," Felicity said. "He's performing the Sacrifice of the One Hundred and Sixty-Nine Souls. It's a thirteen-part ritual that will open a portal to Gibl's world that will remain open. The monster, and whatever else lives in its hellish realm, will be able to come here and feed on as many souls as they want."

I let out a weary sigh. "Okay, so how do we stop it?"

CHAPTER 15

FIRST, WE NEED TO FIND out what stage of the ritual he's at," Felicity said. "I need to see the *Grimoire of Dark Magic*. The ritual is in there. If we can find out where Luke is in the ritual, we might be able to figure out where his next sacrifice to Gibl will take place."

"I'll get the book," Sherry said, heading upstairs.

I sat on the edge of the coffee table and rubbed Felicity's arm gently. "Are you sure you're okay? You look a little shaken up."

"Yes, I'll be fine. It's just that the Sacrifice of the Hundred and Sixty-Nine Souls is dangerous magic. It has the potential to destroy the world. Even in the *Grimoire*, the ritual isn't laid out like most spells; its formula is only revealed in a symbolic story. If Luke manages to pull this off, it's going to be horrible. There will be so many deaths, so much…"

"Hey, listen to me. He's not going to pull it off, okay? We're going to stop him."

She nodded but the worry remained in her eyes.

Sherry returned with the *Grimoire* and put it on the table. The leather cover creaked as she opened it. The pages rustled as she flicked through them.

"There's a section titled *Samuel's Journey*," Felicity said. "The subtitle is *How One Hundred and Sixty-Nine Souls Opened the Gate*."

Sherry flicked past pages containing diagrams of summoning circles and blocks of text. "Got it," she said.

"The ritual is told as a story," Felicity said. "The main character, Samuel, is a practitioner of the dark arts, a worshipper of ancient, evil gods. I think the story begins when he kills someone in his hometown."

Sherry read the first few paragraphs and nodded. "Yeah, it says that Samuel's journey began when he murdered the local wise woman and offered up her soul to the dark gods. Then a demon appeared and told him that to bring the old gods to Earth, he must leave his hometown and sacrifice a total of one hundred and sixty-nine souls."

"That number is used because it's thirteen times thirteen," Felicity said. "It has a lot of power."

"That's what Devon Blackwell said to me. Thirteen times thirteen," I said. "Why the hell don't they ever speak plainly? If she'd told me this ritual was involved, we could have got on it sooner."

"You know what witches are like," Sherry said. "Besides, prophecy doesn't work like that. Devon probably didn't even know what thirteen times thirteen referred to when she said it."

I shrugged. "Yeah, but it still sucks."

Sherry resumed reading. "It says here that the one hundred and sixty-eight remaining souls had to be sacrificed in a certain order. First, Samuel had to sacrifice thirteen virgins." She rolled her eyes. "Well, that's original. Next, thirteen holy men. Then, thirteen sailors. After that, thirteen learned men." She looked up from the text. "The list goes on. Do you want me to read all this?"

I shook my head. "It isn't relevant unless we know where on the list Luke is. And that's even assuming he's following it. That's a lot of killing to carry out."

"He has a monster to help him," Felicity reminded him. "The death of Deirdre Summers could mirror the first killing in the story, the sacrifice of the local wise woman. Deirdre was a librarian so I suppose that fits."

"Loosely," I said.

"The story comes from the Middle Ages," she reminded me. "Luke is finding modern-day equivalents of the victims."

"The story says he left his hometown," Sherry said. "So these murders could have taken place anywhere."

Felicity nodded. "Except they won't look like murders. Deirdre's death looked like a suicide. The others will probably be similar or look like accidents. Luke wouldn't want to draw attention to himself. I'll get my laptop and do a search."

"I'll ask Leon to do that for us," I said. "We need to read the rest of Samuel's story and see if there are any more clues we can use." I got my phone and called Leon.

"Alec," he said when he answered, "what's the problem?"

"Hey, Leon, I need you to do some searching on the internet for me. I'm looking for news reports in the past three years of thirteen people dying at the same time."

"Okay, sounds weird. What incident are you looking for specifically?"

"I'm looking for a lot of them. Get me anything you can find."

"Okay, man. Do you know where these incidents took place?"

I thought about Luke Fairweather's zealous nature and the fact that this ritual was his life's work. He would put as much effort into it as possible to make sure he wasn't caught and stopped before he could complete the sacrifices. He would probably spread the killings over a large area to give himself the best possible chance of staying under the radar of authorities and groups like the Society. "Do a worldwide search," I told Leon.

"Will do. You going to tell me what's going on this time?"

"As soon as I know more, I'll let you in on it," I said.

"Cool. I'll call you back." He ended the call.

I put the phone on the table. "Leon will look into it."

Sherry looked at me incredulously. "Is this someone else you trust with your life?"

"Don't worry, I won't mention your name."

She nodded. "It's just that I came here tonight to look at some books and then leave without being seen. Now, you're getting the whole Scooby Gang involved."

"Don't worry about it," I said. "We need that information." I pointed at the book. "Skip past the list of sacrifices for now. What else does the story say?"

She read farther down the page. "There are descriptions of the killings. Samuel went to a convent in Italy and sacrificed thirteen nuns. I guess those were his virgins. Then, he did the same with thirteen priests. Two months later he went to the docks and sacrificed thirteen sailors. It describes the killings, saying that Samuel was aided by a monstrous servant of the dark gods."

"A servant?" Felicity asked. "So Gibl is just a servant to something even worse?"

Sherry skipped ahead and read a few passages. "It says here that when the ritual is complete, the monstrous servant and its minions will come through the portal to prepare the way for the dark gods."

"So Gibl is just a taste of something worse to come," Felicity said.

"And I assume his minions aren't those cute yellow guys from the movies," I added. "We're going to need help to deal with that many bad guys."

"Cantrell?" Felicity asked.

"I was thinking more along the lines of Leon and Michael, maybe the werewolves, Timothy and Josie, and definitely the Blackwell sisters. Those witches have been vaguebooking the entire time I've been in town. Now it's time they stopped talking in riddles and got their hands dirty."

"Hell, why don't we have a parade and invite the whole town?" Sherry asked sarcastically. She pointed at herself with both hands. "Hello, fugitive from the law here. You invite that many people over and someone is going to talk."

"Do you think the cops are going to be bothered about arresting you when there's a monster trying to eat everyone's souls?"

She shrugged and looked embarrassed. "No, I guess not."

My phone buzzed on the table, the screen displaying Leon's name. I put it on speaker and said, "Hey, Leon, what did you find?"

"Well, it depends on which death of thirteen people you're interested in," he said. "Because there have been quite a few over the past three years."

"Read some out to me. Do you have them in chronological order?"

"Of course. The oldest one I found is the death of thirteen nuns in a fire in a convent in Italy. That happened three years ago, in October. Then, two weeks after that, I have thirteen rabbis who died in a bus crash in France."

"Virgins and holy men," I said. "Just like in the story."

"Story?" Leon asked.

"I'll tell you later. What else have you got?"

"Thirteen sailors died in a boating accident off the coast of Spain in February two years ago."

"He's definitely following the list from Samuel's story," I said. Sherry and Felicity both nodded. "What's the latest incident you have, Leon?" I asked.

"Well, that would be the thirteen people who died in that church near here."

"Yeah, how about the one before that?"

"Thirteen members of various European royal families were lost at sea."

Sherry read down the list in the book. "That's written here as thirteen kings and queens," she said. "After that, Samuel returned to his hometown to carry out the final two sacrifices. The first was the sacrifice of thirteen followers."

"The church at Clara," Felicity said.

"The final sacrifice was of twelve knights." She frowned. "Where's he going to find twelve knights in Dearmont? And why only twelve?"

190

"Because the wise woman who was sacrificed first counted as one soul, so after all those groups of thirteen, there's only twelve left to make one hundred and sixty-nine."

"Okay, but knights?"

The modern-day equivalent would be the police," Felicity said.

Sherry looked dubious. "You think so? You haven't had them chasing your ass for the past seven months."

"It's the police," I said. "But Dearmont doesn't have that large a force. There's Cantrell and maybe, what, four deputies?"

"Five," Felicity said.

"Maybe a different police force, then."

"No, it has to be Dearmont," Felicity said. "The story says Samuel returned to his hometown to carry out the final sacrifices. Luke is following it to the letter and the closest police force to Clara is in Dearmont."

"Hey, man, you going to let me in on what's happening?" Leon asked.

"I'll call you back," I told him. "It's a long story. Are you willing to help us fight some nasties if we need you?"

"You know it."

"Michael too?"

"Of course, he loves using that shotgun every chance he gets."

"Thanks, Leon. I'll call you later." I ended the call and said, "We need to figure out what group of people Luke will substitute for the twelve knights in the final sacrifice."

"Why don't we just follow Luke and see where he goes?" Felicity suggested. "Then we'll be there when he starts the sacrifice."

"He'll go to ground before the big day. This is his life's work so he'll take every precaution to not get caught. Besides, we don't know when he's going to carry out the final sacrifice. We can't tail him forever."

"I think we do know when," Sherry said. "Listen to this. Samuel completed the ritual on the day of his birth so that the occasion also marked the birth of the new world he had created."

"Does it say what day Samuel was born?" I asked.

She pored over the text. "December 25th."

"What?"

"The story is symbolic," Felicity said. "That date would have been chosen as a corruption of Christmas."

"Luke carried out the sacrifice of the followers on December 25th," I said, thinking aloud. "That was probably a symbolic celebration of Samuel's birthday. I guess if he's following the story exactly, he'll perform the final sacrifice on his own birthday."

"Hold on a second," Sherry said. She dug into her box and brought out some handwritten papers. "I did a lot of research on the Fairweather family." She scanned the pages. "So, the Luke Fairweather who was the pastor of the church in 1934 was born on July 19th, 1912."

I felt a coldness in the pit of my stomach. "July 19th is tomorrow."

CHAPTER 16

I PACED BACK AND FORTH, agitated. Time was running out and we still didn't know where Luke and his monster were going to strike. If I thought it would do any good, I'd drive to Clara and burn every house to the ground until I flushed Luke out of hiding but I knew that would be a waste of time—time we didn't have. With the climax of his three-year ritual only a day away, he would be hidden somewhere else, somewhere I'd never find him.

"Twelve knights," I repeated over and over to myself. It had to lead somewhere. If the police angle wasn't feasible because there were only five cops in Dearmont, then there had to be something else.

"We'll go to the island," I said. "That's where Gibl will appear in our realm, so we'll be there waiting for it. We'll send it back to where it came from before Luke can summon it somewhere else."

"That won't work," Felicity said. "You saw that smoke on the crystal image. The monster doesn't become flesh and blood until it's summoned to its final destination. The first summoning brings it into our realm in a ghost-like state. But if it is going to be summoned elsewhere, while it waits on the island, it can't be touched, never mind killed. When Luke casts the second summoning spell at the location of the sacrifice, the creature appears there in a solid form. Then it fades away, as Sherry saw in the church." She sighed. "Only this time it won't fade away. It will be here forever."

"Only if Luke sacrifices twelve knights," I said. "We can stop that from happening."

"And how are we going to do that?" Sherry asked, "When we don't have a clue where this sacrifice is going down? Twelve knights might mean twelve members of the Knights of Columbus for all we know."

She was right. We had no idea who the intended victims were and going over it again and again wasn't going to get us anywhere. "The one thing we do know," I said, "is that the sacrifice will take place tomorrow. We don't know exactly where it's going to happen but it will be somewhere in or around Dearmont. So how can we use that to our advantage?"

"I guess we could patrol the area and wait for something to happen," Sherry said.

That gave me an idea. "We don't have to patrol the area to know when something happens," I said. "Someone else can do it for us." I called Leon again. "Leon," I said when he answered, "do you still have that police scanner in your RV?"

"Of course. I've got a whole bunch of them. Not that there's anything worth listening to around here."

"Great. What are you doing tomorrow?"

"Nothing that can't be rearranged."

"Okay, you and Michael come over to my place in the morning. Bring a police scanner and your weapons."

"We'll be there, man."

"Thanks, I'll explain everything when you get here." I ended the call.

"What was that all about?" Felicity asked.

"We know something is going down tomorrow but we don't know where. So we monitor the police channel and wait until they get a call. As soon as we hear something that sounds like the ritual taking place, we get over there fast."

Sherry nodded. "I guess that makes sense."

"It's the only thing we can do," I said. "I'll get everyone to come over here in the morning. Then we wait until Luke makes his move."

"I'll bring some food over," Felicity offered. "We don't know when Luke will perform the ritual. It might not be until nighttime."

"I think it'll be earlier than that," I said. "It's his birthday and I'm sure he won't want to wait to open his presents."

Sherry yawned. "It's getting late. I should be going. What time do you want me here in the morning?"

"Do you have a place to stay?" I asked her.

She got up out of the easy chair and stretched. "I have a place to stay. What do you think I've been doing for the past seven months, sleeping in the woods?" She winked at me to tell me she was joking. "I'll leave you two lovebirds alone. See you in the morning, bright and early."

I followed her down to the front door and opened it for her. She stepped out into the night and turned to face me, her expression serious. "You seem like a good man, Alec. I think my decision to trust you was the right one."

"It was," I said. "When this is all over, I'll call my father and get him to take you back into the Society."

"Is he as trustworthy as his son?"

I sighed. "He can be trusted with Society business. And I know he isn't a member of the Midnight Cabal."

She pursed her lips. "That sounds very matter-of-fact. Not exactly a glowing recommendation from a family member."

"No, well, he got some witches to do bad things to me when I was younger."

She raised her eyebrows. "Ouch, that sounds painful."

"Don't let it influence your decision about whether to come back to the Society or not. As far as my dad's concerned, the Society comes before everything else. He won't want to lose a good investigator."

Sherry smiled. "Thanks, Alec. I'll think about it. After tomorrow, we may be living in some sort of end-of-the-world monster apocalypse anyway." She waved and walked away.

I closed the door and went back up to the living room. Felicity was clearing away the dishes.

"You don't have to do that," I said.

"I don't mind." She took the dishes into the kitchen and began loading the dishwasher. There was a nervous energy in the way she moved.

"Is everything okay?" I asked.

She closed the dishwasher and stood to face me. "Yes, everything's fine. I'm just scared about tomorrow." Her glasses had slid down her nose slightly. She pushed them back up. "I don't want to be alone tonight, Alec. The thought of going back to my house fills me with dread."

"That's not a problem, you can stay here."

She smiled nervously. "Really?"

"Of course. Do you want to take one of the spare bedrooms?" Chivalry wasn't dead. Hell, maybe I was one of the twelve knights the dark gods wanted to eat.

She swallowed. "I'd rather be with you if that's all right. I don't mean…in that way. I just want to be close to you."

"That's not a problem."

"I still don't think I'll get a wink of sleep," she said, relaxing a little. "I'm too worried about tomorrow."

"Me too," I told her. "But if I don't sleep tonight, I'll feel bad tomorrow and I hate fighting monsters when I'm tired. It just makes me cranky."

She laughed.

"You go ahead. I'm just going to lock up down here and raise the level of the wards," I said.

Felicity nodded. "See you in a minute." She ascended the stairs.

I went into the living room and sat on the floor, closing my eyes and mentally connecting to the wards that protected the house. Wards were one of the first things I'd learned at the Academy of Shadows and I'd spent weeks warding everything I could, from my dorm room to my lunchbox.

The wards around the house were adequate for keeping out vampires, demons, faeries, and mundane thieves, but they could still be defeated by another Society member or a powerful magician like Luke Fairweather. I didn't think Luke was going to attack us tonight but it was better to be safe than sorry.

I visualized the glowing green circles and glyphs that surrounded the house and recited a spell that would strengthen them for tonight. It wasn't a good idea to place strong wards around the house permanently because the stronger ones burned with a powerful magical energy that attracted any beings nearby that were sensitive to magic, especially lesser beings that existed on the astral plane and sought energy to feed on.

So I usually stuck to the "slow burners" that were powerful enough to keep most things out but not so powerful as to turn my house into a magical beacon.

For tonight, though, I would feel better knowing that Felicity and I were safe inside a powerful magical barrier. In my mind's eye, the symbols of protection glowed brighter around the house. I kept the visualization at the front of my mind for a couple of seconds but it wavered when my thoughts turned to Felicity. She was upstairs in my bedroom, probably in my bed by now.

I pushed that thought away and went back to the wards again, continuing where I'd left off. When they were at full strength, I opened my eyes and stood up. Despite the wards being at full strength, I still locked the front door. Then I turned out all the downstairs lights and went upstairs.

The bedroom door was slightly open, the room beyond dark. I knocked lightly. "Can I come in?"

"Of course," Felicity said.

I entered the room and waited a couple of seconds for my eyes to adjust to the darkness. Felicity was in bed, the cream-colored sheet pulled over her body. I undressed quickly, stripping down to my boxers. The night was hot, despite the cool air being pumped through the vents.

I pulled the sheet aside and slid into bed next to Felicity, pulling the sheet back over us. She was wearing a pale pink bra and panties. She turned to me, her dark eyes searching my face in the darkness. Her glasses were on the nightstand and their absence from her face made Felicity seem vulnerable somehow.

Our mouths met in a long, slow, gentle kiss. I placed a hand on her waist. Her skin felt hot. Her own hand stroked over my arm, her fingers tracing the outline of my muscles.

When our mouths parted, Felicity whispered to me, "We need to get some sleep."

"Yeah, we do," I said.

I reluctantly took my hand from her waist but she stopped me, placing her hand over mine. "Leave it there," she whispered. "It's nice." She snuggled up against me and buried her head against my chest.

I held her close and shut my eyes, sleep taking me faster than I had expected. I let myself drift into its grip. I needed to be alert tomorrow, but for now I could relax and allow myself to dream.

CHAPTER 17

I AWOKE THE NEXT MORNING to find myself alone in the bed. Pale light crept in through the window and when I checked the clock on the nightstand, it told me it was six thirty. I sat up. Felicity's glasses were gone from the nightstand, her peach blouse and jeans gone from the chair where they'd been neatly folded last night.

Without bothering to get dressed, I went downstairs and made coffee. While it was brewing, I went down to the basement and selected a sword and a pistol crossbow. I went back upstairs and leaned the weapons against the wall by the front door.

I checked the bandage around the bullet wound. It was still tight and the only pain I felt in my side was a dull ache. I was good to go.

A half hour later, I was showered, dressed and on my second cup of coffee when the front door opened and Felicity came inside. She was dressed in jeans and a dark green T-shirt. Her dark hair was piled up on her head in its usual style. "Oh, you're awake," she said when she saw me.

"I am indeed," I said, raising my coffee cup by way of a greeting. "Did you sleep well last night?"

She smiled prettily. "Yes, very well. You?"

"Like the dead," I said.

"That's probably not the best choice of phrase for today," she said, coming into the kitchen. "I've put some cinnamon bakes in my oven. If you're inviting people around, they might as well have something to eat."

"Sure," I said. "You want a drink?"

"Tea, please. Thanks. I'll make it."

I watched her as she made herself a cup of tea. Last night's closeness seemed to have vanished with the night. I wanted nothing more than to take Felicity in my arms and kiss her but she was back to being her business-like self again.

"Is everything okay, Felicity?"

"Yes, of course. I'm just so nervous about today. I'd feel better if we knew more about Luke Fairweather's plans."

"Yeah, me too, but we have to do the best we can with the little we have."

"I know." She took a sip of the hot tea. "I wonder what time Leon will arrive?"

"Early," I said. "He wants to know what's happening. He's probably on his way here right now."

She laughed. "Yes, he is eager to help. It's nice." The last two words reminded me of when she'd told me to keep my hand on her waist last night. "How are you going to convince the Blackwell sisters to help us?" she asked.

I hadn't really thought about it. The sisters didn't do anything unless they got something in return. I already owed them a favor for the werewolf locator spell they'd cast for me. What would they charge to fight the servant of a dark god and his minions? I wasn't ready to trade my soul just yet. "I'll just tell them the situation," I said to Felicity. "If we don't defeat Gibl, all their customers will be eaten by monsters. That should motivate them."

There was a knock on the front door. I answered it to find Leon and Michael standing outside. They were both dressed in the same black garb they always seemed to wear when they were about to go into action.

Even though Leon was a young black man who had made a fortune in the computer tech world, and Michael was a white British man in his sixties who worked as Leon's butler, there seemed to be a strong friendship between the two of them.

"You going to tell us what's going on now, Alec?" Leon asked as he stepped into the house. Michael followed, nodding silently to me in greeting.

"Felicity will tell you everything," I said. "I have to visit a couple of witches."

I pulled on my boots and asked Felicity to call Timothy and Josie, the werewolves I locked away every full moon. Grabbing the keys to the Caprice, I went outside and got into the car. It was another warm morning and the temperature would probably rise as the day wore on.

I backed out of the driveway, being careful to avoid Leon's RV parked on the street. Five minutes later, I was driving down Main Street. When I reached Blackwell Books, I cursed. The place wasn't open yet. I parked outside and went to the door, peering through the glass at the dark interior of the bookshop.

Even though it was early, the witches might still be in there. They ran a mail order business from the back room so maybe they arrived early to sort out that side of things. I knocked on the glass and searched the darkness between the bookshelves for a sign of movement. Nothing.

I turned to leave, intending to call the witches later, but then I saw them on the sidewalk, approaching me. They both wore their trademark black Victorian dresses and Devon held a black lace parasol above their heads.

"Alec, you beat us here," Victoria said when they reached me. "We know why you're here."

"You do?" I asked, surprised. I wasn't sure why I was still surprised by anything the Blackwell sisters said.

"You want our help. Devon had a dream last night."

"There's a monster," Devon said. "I saw it coming through a portal. And I saw you standing outside the bookshop before we opened."

"So here we are," Victoria added.

"And you'll help?"

"Of course." She made it sound as if they hadn't asked me for some sort of payment every time I'd asked for their help.

"We're all gathering at my place," I said. "Do you have a car?"

"Yes, but it's such a nice day we decided to walk," Victoria said.

So Devon's prophetic vision hadn't told them they'd need a car. "Do you want to go get your car or do you want me to drive you to my house?"

"You can drive us," Devon said.

"Fine." I got into the Caprice and they both climbed into the back seat. As I drove back to the house, I told them about Luke Fairweather and the ritual he was carrying out. Every now and then, the witches would mutter, "That's terrible," or, "How awful," but other than that, they listened quietly.

When we got to the house, Devon said, "Your house is very well-protected, Alec."

"Yeah, you can't be too careful these days." I invited them inside and introduced them to Leon and Michael. The police scanner sat on the coffee table, picking up the occasional conversation between the dispatcher and one of the deputies, but nothing else. It was a slow day for law enforcement.

The house smelled of apple bakes. Felicity had set out two plates of the baked goodies on the coffee table. Victoria took a bite of one and said to Felicity, "These are delicious. You must give me the recipe sometime."

Felicity nodded but looked a little uncomfortable.

"Did you call Timothy and Josie?" I asked her.

"Yes, they're on their way."

"No sign of Sherry?"

She shook her head.

"She was concerned about showing her face," I said. "Maybe she lost her nerve."

"I'm sure she'll be here," Felicity said. "She knows how important this is."

A short hiss of static sounded on the police scanner, followed by the female dispatcher's voice. "All cars. All cars. We've had multiple reports of gunmen at Dearmont Lake. Shots fired."

Cantrell's voice said, "Goddamn hunters. Amy, what's your location?"

"I'm near the lake," Amy said. "I'll check it out."

"That could be something to do with Luke," Felicity said.

"Maybe."

Everyone sitting around the police scanner was leaning in, waiting to hear Amy's report.

When it came, Amy's voice was tense. "I need backup. There are at least three gunmen at the docks. They're firing at my vehicle." There was a pause and then the sound of shots. "I'm returning fire but I need backup now!"

Cantrell said, "Everybody get down to the docks. Dispatch, call the state police. Tell them we need urgent assistance."

Now it all made sense. "Twelve knights" did refer to the police after all. Luke had set up a situation that gave the sheriff no option other than to call the state police for assistance so there would be more than six police officers at the docks.

They were rushing into a trap.

And twelve of them would be sacrificed in a black magic ritual.

CHAPTER 18

THE CAPRICE SPED ALONG THE highway. The Blackwell sisters were in the back seat, talking quietly to each other. Felicity rode shotgun, looking nervously out through the windshield at the road ahead.

Leon's RV was close behind us, with Michael at the wheel and Leon in the passenger seat checking their shotguns.

"Felicity, call Timothy and Josie and tell them to meet us at the docks." I wished I had a number for Sherry. She was a trained fighter like me and her being here could be the difference between us winning or losing this battle.

Felicity jabbed at her phone and put it to her ear. After a couple of minutes, she said, "There's no answer from Timothy." She tried again and said, "No answer from Josie either."

Great. So there were six of us against a black magician, a monster, and the monster's minions. I didn't like those odds.

I turned off the highway and on to the road the led to the lake. Six police cruisers were parked in the parking lot, their lights flashing. Crouched behind the vehicles were Cantrell, Amy, and four other officers. Their guns were drawn but they weren't firing at anything.

I drove the Caprice around the police vehicles and parked behind them. Michael did the same with the RV.

When I got out of the car, Cantrell shouted, "Get out of here, Harbinger." His face was red and at first I thought that was from anger but then I realized he was sunburned from when we'd taken the boat to the island and he'd fallen asleep.

"I can't do that, Sheriff. You need to get on the radio and call off the state police. When they get here, all hell is going to break loose."

"It's already broken loose," he said. "Maybe you haven't noticed, but we're being shot at."

"There's a guy somewhere around here who needs twelve police officers on the scene so he can cast a spell that could destroy the world."

"What the hell are you talking about?" He held up a huge hand. "No, don't tell me. I don't want to know."

I turned to Amy. "Can you help me out here?"

She shrugged. "What do you want me to do?"

"Convince your dad to call off the state police. Trust me, things are going to get a lot worse if they come here."

She hesitated, uncertainty in her eyes. "Alec, I don't think I can…"

"Do you trust me?" I asked her.

"Of course she doesn't," Cantrell answered for her. "You can't be trusted, Harbinger."

"Dad, maybe he's right," she said. "Maybe we should listen to him."

Cantrell wavered slightly. For all his pig-headed stubbornness, he knew I was no charlatan. He'd seen a glimpse of my world with his own eyes. He said, "Are you going to tell me what's going on here?"

"I just did. If the state police arrive, their presence will enable an evil magician to cast a spell that will bring that monster we saw into this realm permanently. And the monster isn't even the worst thing that's going to come here. It's going to bring its minions and they're going to prepare our world for the arrival of the dark gods. I'm pretty sure we don't want to ever meet those guys."

Cantrell sighed resignedly. "Okay, I'll call off the state troopers. We'll apprehend the shooters ourselves." He went around to the open door of his car and reached in to get his radio. He told the dispatcher to cancel the state police.

"What now?" Amy asked me.

"I need to find one very pissed magician," I said. "Sooner or later, he's going to realize that he doesn't have the ingredients he needs to complete a spell that's taken him three years to cast."

"Sucks for him," she said.

"Yeah."

"Never mind that," Cantrell said. "Who the hell are those gunmen holed up in that shack?"

"They're members of the Fairweather family," I said. "Sent here to cause enough trouble that you'd call the state police. The magician needs twelve knights here so he can sacrifice them for his ritual. The Dearmont police force isn't big enough. There are only six of you." My voice trailed off as I made a realization.

I turned to the Caprice and the RV. There were six of us. Felicity, Michael, Leon, the Blackwell sisters, and me. All six of us had come here to stop evil and save the world. Wasn't that knightly behavior? "Oh, shit," I said. "Luke doesn't need the state police. We're the other six knights."

A low rumbling rolled across the lake like thunder and out on Whitefish Island, a column of thick, black smoke rose into the air. The final part of the ritual had begun.

CHAPTER 19

I PULLED OPEN THE CAPRICE'S trunk and took out my sword and pistol crossbow. A quiver of bolts went onto my belt, along with a knife.

Felicity came around to the trunk. "Alec, what's your plan?"

"Kill anything that moves," I said.

"Good plan," Leon said from behind me. He and Michael had shotguns slung over their shoulders and a backpack full of shells. "Where do you want us?"

Creatures began to emerge from the lake. They were similar to frogs but at least six-feet long. Their eyes fixed on us with malevolent stares and the creatures crawled toward us on their clawed feet.

"Over there," I told Leon. "Deal with those frog monsters."

He and Michael ran toward the edge of the lake and began firing. The frog monsters emitted high-pitched squeals when they were hit and, when they died, their bodies deflated and became puddles of green, slimy flesh.

"I need to get to the island," I told Felicity.

"I'm coming with you." She reached into the trunk and took out a second sword.

"Felicity, you haven't been trained to use that."

"There's no time to argue, Alec. Let's go."

She was right about there being no time to argue. I needed to get to the island and close the portal there before more creatures came through it.

The sheriff and his deputies had turned their attention to the frog monsters, firing at them while still using the patrol cars as cover. I was going to have to deal with the Fairweather family if I wanted to get a boat. The shack they were in belonged to one of the boat hire businesses. I couldn't get to the boats without getting past the Fairweathers.

"Stay behind me," I told Felicity. I loaded the pistol crossbow as we made our way over to the shack.

One of the bearded brothers appeared from behind the shack, a revolver in his hands. I grabbed Felicity and threw myself to the ground, taking her with me. A shot rang out and I heard the bullet scream through the air over our bodies. I got the pistol crossbow into position and fired. The bolt hit the Fairweather brother in the chest. He fell backward and landed heavily on the ground, dust pluming up around his body.

The other brother appeared, brandishing a rifle. The sight of his brother made him hesitate slightly and that was all the time I needed to load another bolt into the crossbow as I scrambled to my feet. I shot him before he'd even aimed at us. My bolt punctured his shoulder and he dropped the rifle so he could clutch at the wound, crying out.

His cries brought the old lady out from the shack. She had a shotgun and it was already in firing position, braced against her shoulder and aimed right at me. I didn't have time to reload the pistol crossbow. I handed it to Felicity and drew my sword, knowing I didn't have time to get to the old woman before she shot me but still willing to give it a try.

The old woman cackled as she was about to pull the trigger.

A crossbow bolt suddenly appeared, sticking out of her chest. The old woman looked down at the bolt lodged in her body, her face a mask of surprise. She dropped to the ground and the shotgun went clattering into the grass.

I looked around. A red Mustang was parked on the road that led to the parking lot and standing on its roof was Sherry, crossbow in hand. She gave me a thumbs-up and dropped gracefully from the car roof to the ground before running over to us.

"What took you so long?" I asked her.

She put on a mock offended look. "I thought my timing was perfect."

I looked at the old lady's body. "I guess it was. Thanks."

"Don't mention it. What's the plan?"

"We need to get to the island. Luke is there. Now that he's cast the spell and expended all that energy, he should be weakened. The monsters have to kill all twelve of us for the ritual to succeed and the portal to stay open, so we need to stay alive."

"I hear that," Sherry said.

We moved toward the dock. When we reached Woody's Boat Hire, I kicked the door open and grabbed the keys for the *Princess of the Lake*. Felicity and I got on board while Sherry untied the boat. By the time she'd done that and jumped on board herself, I had the engine started. The smell of gasoline rose into the air as I gunned the engine and piloted us away from the dock and out onto the lake.

Thick, dark smoke was still belching from the center of Whitefish Island. I looked over at the parking lot where the police and Leon and Michael were keeping the frog monsters at bay with their guns. The green-skinned creatures swarmed from the water and it wouldn't be long before ammo supplies became depleted and the people in the parking lot would have to find other ways to kill the monsters.

The boat suddenly shuddered and the engine cut out.

"What the hell was that?" Sherry asked. "Did we hit rocks or something?"

"No, it wasn't rocks," I said, readying my sword.

The water all around us erupted and I saw flashes of green as frog monsters leaped into the boat. One of them lashed out at me with its claws. I stepped back and swung the sword, severing the monster's arm. It squealed and shot its snake-like pink tongue at me. I deflected it with the flat of my blade and then moved forward, burying my sword in the monster's chest. It deflated into a puddle of green slime.

I looked up in time to see Felicity gracefully swinging her sword at a frog monster's head. The creature struggled for a second before becoming a pool of green goo at her feet.

Sherry was hacking and slashing at two monsters at the rear of the boat. No sooner had she killed them than three more leaped on board. "Alec, get us out of here!" she shouted.

Felicity joined the fray, stabbing her sword through a frog monster's chest so hard that the point of the glowing blade went all the way through the creature's body and came out of its back.

I tried the engine again. It started and I slammed the throttle forward. The boat accelerated over the water, kicking up spray from the hull. A frog monster managed to clamber on board before we reached full speed. I swung my sword at its head and decapitated it.

As we got closer to the island, the smell of sulfur hung in the air. It came from the noxious black smoke that continued to belch from the trees into the sky.

"I guess that's the portal," I said.

Felicity came to the control console and peered at the smoke. Her glasses had slid down her nose lightly and her forehead was beaded with perspiration. Her hair had come loose from the pins that kept it piled up on her head and now it tumbled over her shoulders. A thick strand clung to Felicity's cheek, curling toward her mouth, and another snaked around her neck, kept in place by the moisture in her skin.

"That's the portal," she said. "Luke will be somewhere in there, keeping it open with his magic until the sacrifice is complete."

I looked back toward the parking lot. "I don't think that's going to happen. If Luke's original plan had gone ahead and we hadn't been ready to act, he probably would have killed twelve cops and completed the ritual. But now half of his intended victims are people who have had experience fighting supernatural creatures."

"He hasn't used his most dangerous weapon yet," Felicity reminded me.

That was true. Gibl seemed to be holding back, letting its minions do all the work. If completing this ritual meant that it could roam our realm, I would have expected it to be more involved in the fighting.

I pulled back on the throttle and guided the *Princess* to the little rickety dock. Sherry stepped out onto the wooden slats and tied the boat securely. I heard another boat and turned to see the Blackwell sisters sailing toward us in a boat identical to ours. They stood together at the control console and waved at us as if they were out on the lake for a pleasurable morning excursion.

We waited while they landed at the dock and stepped onto the island to join us.

"We thought we'd be more useful here than back there," Victoria said. "Guns are quite distasteful."

"What can you do about this?" I indicated the column of smoke.

They conferred for a moment and then Devon said, "We can probably close it, given enough time."

"We'll get to work on the proper spell," Victoria said.

I wasn't going to wait around while they did that so I strode forward into the portal, followed by Felicity and Sherry. The blue glow from our swords illuminated the black smoke. I had no idea which direction I was traveling in or even if I was going around in circles. I concentrated on moving in a straight line, hoping that I'd lead us out of the sulfurous darkness. The smoke stung my eyes and clung to my skin and made breathing difficult.

Finally, after long minutes of wandering in the smoke, we broke free of it and found ourselves in the clearing with the tree-stump altar. I breathed in a deep lungful of air and rubbed my skin where the smoke was clinging to me.

There was no sign of Luke. "Where the hell is he?" I said, frustrated. "And where is Gibl?"

"We'll have to go back," Sherry said. "We're wasting time here."

I nodded in agreement and set off into the smoke again. When we came out of the other side, the Blackwell sisters were still talking to each other. "I don't see any spell casting taking place," I told them.

"We're working on it," Victoria said.

I looked over the water toward the parking lot and a chill settled between my shoulder blades. Gibl was in the lot, towering above everything, even the tallest trees. It looked like an enormous frog except that it had many eyes and mouths all over its body. The eyes were frog eyes and they seemed to stare in every direction. The mouths were lined with sharp, needle-like teeth and each had a long tongue that flickered back and forth like a snake seeking prey.

Gibl raised one huge arm and brought it down on top of a police cruiser, smashing the vehicle as if it were a toy. One of the deputies had been hiding behind the car. He ran for the road that led to the highway, only to be caught by a long tongue that shot out from one of the mouths on Gibl's stomach and dragged him into the waiting maw, screaming.

In the trees where Cantrell and I had seen the vision of Deirdre Summer's death, Luke stood watching as the monster went on the rampage.

"He must have had a summoning circle set up over there," Felicity said. "He guessed that we'd come to the island to look for him and he used that to split the group up."

I jerked my thumb in the direction of the Blackwell sisters. "What happens if those two actually manage to close the portal and Gibl is on this side of it?"

"It will be dragged back through. Only when the *Hundred and Sixty-Nine Souls* ritual is complete can the portal remain open and Gibl remain on this side of it. Until then, the portal is like any other. If it closes, it drags everything that shouldn't be on this side back to the other side."

"Get that thing closed as soon as possible," I told the Blackwell sisters before getting back on board the *Princess* with Felicity and Sherry. We set off back the way we had come, swords ready in case the frog monsters tried to board us again.

We got back to the dock without incident. In the parking lot, the battle raged on. Cantrell and his remaining deputies were shooting at frog monsters and moving between cars while Gibl smashed the vehicles and sent his many tongues shooting out at his prey. Leon and Michael were kneeling on the trail by the lake's edge, firing their shotguns at Gibl. Some of the many frog eyes were leaking a translucent slime and I assumed they had been shot at and hit.

I glanced over at the island. The smoke was still rising. What the hell were those witches doing?

To reach Luke, I needed to get past Gibl. That wasn't going to be easy. I moved forward, ready to slash at anything that came shooting in my direction, whether it was one of Gibl's tongues or its huge, clawed hand.

The monster saw us and turned its head in our direction. I wished I'd had more time to practice my magic. The only trick in my arsenal was throwing a blast of energy that depleted my strength entirely. If I tried that now, I would be helpless for the rest of this fight. And I had no guarantee that the blast would even hurt Gibl.

It raised its massive hand and brought it down toward us. I stepped back and instinctively raised my free hand as if to ward off the blow. A blue shield of magical energy appeared above me, formed from a spiderweb of glowing magical circles and symbols. Gibl's hand crashed down on it and the shield held. The monster raised its hand quickly as if stung.

Okay, that was new. I just hoped the shield didn't drain as much energy as a magical blast because I wanted to make sure I had plenty of gas left in the tank when I came face to face with Luke.

"What the hell was that?" Sherry asked.

"It's a long story," I said.

"I think I can guess. The witches that did bad things to you when you were younger?"

"Yeah." I moved forward, desperate to get past Gibl and face Luke in case I was going to collapse sometime soon.

One of the deputies stepped forward from behind a car and unloaded a magazine into Gibl's body. Either he had seen Gibl's reaction to touching my magical shield and decided to take the opportunity to get some shots in, or he was just playing hero.

Gibl turned on him and brought its hand down, crushing the deputy and the car in a wreck of metal, glass, flesh, and bone.

I ran for the woods, Felicity and Sherry close behind. We reached the trees and kept moving, slowing our pace to avoid tripping over fallen branches or roots hidden beneath the undergrowth. I veered left to hit the trail and when my feet touched the hard-packed earth there, I increased my pace again. Luke was not going to get away, I would make sure of that.

When I saw him, he was standing at the edge of the lake, by the rocks where Deirdre Summers had entered the water and begun the three-year ritual that was ending, one way or the other, today.

Luke grinned when he saw us. "Harbinger, you've fallen for every misdirection and trap I've put in your path. First you went to the island, splitting up your group, and now you're standing exactly where I want you: right in front of me, ready to be slain. Twelve souls will be sacrificed to Gibl this day and the portal between our

223

world and that of the dark gods will remain open, heralding a new age of darkness and destruction. Your death will be part of the foundation of that new age."

"Yeah, I think I'll pass."

His face grew furious. A blue glow began to crackle in the air around his hands. He raised them and flung them forward. A bright blue ball of energy shot toward me.

I raised the magical shield. The ball crashed into it and then dissipated.

Luke looked shocked. "No, this can't be. You have to die, Harbinger!"

"Like I said, I'll pass." I summoned up my own magical blast, feeling it rise up through my body and down along my arms. I released it in Luke's direction. Green lines of energy formed complex magical shapes in the air around my hands, shapes that I now thought were connected to the inscriptions on my bones, before massing together into a single ball of energy that shot forward.

Luke raised a shield of his own, a plain glowing blue wall. My energy ball hit it and sparked into thousands of glowing green shards.

I had to strike now before I became weak. I ran forward, preparing to swing my sword at his neck. He backed away, his feet going into the water, and raised another magical shield. The enchanted blade sliced through the shield in a shower of blue sparks. Luke stumbled backward into the lake, out of the sword's reach.

Thunder rumbled over the lake, just as it had when the portal had been opened. I looked at Whitefish Island. The smoke was disappearing. The witches had finally taken action and closed the portal.

"No," Luke groaned. "No, it can't be."

"Looks like your three-year ritual is ended," I told him. "That'll teach you to mess with knights."

His eyes went to Gibl. The monster looked over at the closing portal, then at Luke. It advanced on him, obviously pissed that its ticket to our realm was now void. It had worked with Luke for all that time and now Luke had let it down.

A long pink tongue shot out from one of the multitude of mouths and wound around Luke's arm. Another grabbed his leg. I stepped back, out of the way, as another tongue snaked around Luke's neck.

His eyes bulged. "No, help me. Harbinger, help me."

Gibl began to be sucked toward the island and the closing portal, dragging Luke with it. As they were pulled across the surface of the lake by the strong magical force, along with the frog monsters that were still alive, Luke began to scream. He was pulled into the smoke along with the monsters and then the smoke began to recede quickly, disappearing completely within seconds.

I turned from the lake and said to Felicity and Sherry, "Let's go home."

"She's not going anywhere." Cantrell's voice came from the trail. He was standing there with his handgun in his hands, the muzzle pointed at Sherry. He was sweaty and dirty and there was blood on his uniform. The grim expression on his face told me he couldn't be reasoned with.

Amy appeared on the trail behind him. "Dad, what are you doing?" Her uniform was also bloody and disheveled. There was a sadness in her eyes that hadn't been there before today. She had lost friends and colleagues in the parking lot.

"I'm doing what I've dreamed of doing ever since your mother was killed," Cantrell said. "I'm taking my revenge."

Despite having a gun pointed at her, Sherry was calm. "Sheriff, I'm glad you're standing in front of me talking about your wife because there's something I have to tell you, something you are unaware of. Mary wasn't involved with that church in the way you think she was. She was working with me to bring it down. You see, she wanted to be just like you and your daughter there. She wanted to make a difference."

Cantrell's hands wavered slightly. "What? What are you saying?"

"I'm saying that Mary wanted to do something good. She was so proud of you and your daughter and she wanted to make you proud of her."

"Of course I was proud of her," he said, his voice softening. "I loved her."

"Yes, she knew that. But she thought of you and Amy as special and she wanted to be special too. That's why she set her heart on taking down that church at Clara. She knew something was wrong there, something evil, and she wanted to make it right. Even when I told her she couldn't be a part of my investigation, she wouldn't take no for an answer because she knew she was doing something good."

Tears had begun to well in Amy's eyes. The sheriff looked sad and confused. He lowered the gun slightly.

Sherry looked at him with compassion in her eyes. "Sir, your wife died a hero and I have wanted to tell you that for such a very long time."

Cantrell dropped to one knee, as if the exertion of the day had suddenly caught up with him. "Mary," he said pitifully.

Sherry walked over to him and crouched in front of him. She put a hand on his shoulder. "Today, we finished what she started. I think she'd be pleased with that."

Cantrell nodded slowly, his eyes gazing at the ground as he tried to comprehend what he had just been told. Amy went to him and put her arm around him. She was crying freely. When Sherry stood up, Amy mouthed, "Thank you," to her.

Sherry nodded and walked up to the trail. Felicity and I followed. We walked in silence along the trail to the parking lot where a battle with a monster had once raged but now only broken things remained.

CHAPTER 20

TWO DAYS LATER, FELICITY, SHERRY, and I stood on the runway at Bangor International Airport, next to one of the Society's private jets. Two Society security guards dressed in black suits and wearing aviator sunglasses flanked the metal steps that led up to the plane's open door.

Felicity had called my father and explained Sherry's plight and he had been understanding, as I knew he would be, and said that she could go and work for the Society in London. The recent expulsion of a number of members found to be spies for the Midnight Cabal meant there was a shortage of staff working from the London headquarters, and an investigator of Sherry's high standard was more than welcome.

"Well, I guess this is it," Sherry said, dropping her carry-on bag on the tarmac and giving me a hug. "Thanks for everything, Alec."

"No problem. Be careful and don't go getting into fights you can't win."

She arched an eyebrow at me. "Fights I can't win? What the hell is that supposed to mean?"

"Well, when you and I fought, you had to quit. Fighting against me, that's okay because I'm an understanding guy, but not everyone will be so lenient."

"Lenient? I could have kicked your ass."

"You said, 'I quit,' and that's when we stopped."

"I said 'time out.' There's a difference."

I shrugged noncommittally. Sherry knew I was just pulling her leg. She looked at me with an incredulous look and then we both burst out laughing.

"The next time I see you," she said, "there's going to be a rematch. Then we'll see who quits." She hugged Felicity. "You take care, honey. And hold on to this one, he's a keeper." Then she added, "But don't tell him I said that."

Felicity grinned. "Have a safe journey."

"Don't you worry about me," Sherry said. "I'll send you a postcard from the Tower of London." She picked up her bag and went up the steps to the plane. At the top, she turned around and said to me, "Harbinger, you're one of the good guys. I hope we meet again." With that, she disappeared into the plane.

Felicity and I walked back through the terminals to where I'd parked the Miracle Car. We'd given that name to June and Earl's Caprice because when we got to the parking lot where the battle with Gibl had taken place, nearly every vehicle was scratched, dented, or crushed. Most of the police cruisers had been destroyed and Leon's RV had been crushed at one end. But the Caprice had been sitting in the middle of all the action and hadn't suffered a single scratch.

We got into the car and Felicity said, "Perhaps the sheriff will soften a bit now."

I grunted. "I doubt it. I'm sure he'll still be a pain in the ass." I started the Caprice, drove us out of the airport, and headed for I-95.

Felicity shook her head. "You're always so cynical, Alec."

"I told you before, being cynical has kept me alive this long."

"No, you said being suspicious has kept you alive this long."

"Cynicism and suspicion go well together."

She relaxed back in her seat. The sun flooding in through the windows lit her up as if she were on fire. "Well, I'm not going to let your mood affect me. We've just completed a case and there's nothing bad happening at the moment. That makes a welcome change and I am going to enjoy it."

I said nothing. There was always something bad happening somewhere. The Midnight Cabal was gaining power. I was indebted to a faerie queen. There were marks on my bones that had been put there with my father's consent. I knew the location of the Spear of Destiny, an artifact so powerful that nobody should ever get their hands on it. Just the fact that it existed meant there was potential for bad things to happen.

"You look serious," Felicity said, "What are you thinking about?"

"Destiny."

"Do you believe in destiny?"

Keeping my eyes locked on the road ahead, I said, "I believe that sometimes we can't escape it."

THE END

The Harbinger P.I. Series

LOST SOUL

BURIED MEMORY

DARK MAGIC

DEAD GROUND (coming soon)

41290502R00142

Made in the USA
Middletown, DE
05 April 2019